Greenwood Gone: Henry's Story

Sioux Roslawski

Editor-911 Kids

Author proceeds from <u>Greenwood Gone: Henry's Story</u> will be donated to the people of Greenwood, OK.

Cover design by Jessica Esfahani

Printed in the United States of America

Editor-911 Kids,
an imprint of Editor-911 Books
P.O. Box 313
Eureka, MO 63025

Dedication

To all the Henrys (and their families), whose lives
were taken by the Tulsa Race Massacre.
May we someday learn from our history and stop
repeating it.
.

Tuesday, May 31, 1921, 4:00 p.m.

Thwok! Carl's pitch hit my glove like a bullet. That one stung like the dickens. I didn't want to wince, but I guess my eyes gave it away. I couldn't help it.

"I got you! I got you that time. I know I did!" he said as he jabbed his finger towards me.

I shook my hand, trying to shake off the sting. "Well, wait til you feel the one I'm about to throw you. It's gonna tear your glove clean off your hand."

It was one of those perfect days for playing outside. The sky was nothing but blue—all the clouds had been chased away. It was warm, but not so hot to make the sweat trickle down my shirt. Once in a while, there was even a breeze whispering past.

Carl and I only had a couple of hours. As soon as Daddy got home from work, Mama would open up the screen door and holler for me to get inside. The same thing happened up and down the block. When I heard Mama call out, "Henry!" I hurried. I liked my rear end too much to dawdle and risk being the target of my mother's anger. Nobody's mama wanted to wait dinner while a game of catch was getting finished.

I started to wind up but stopped. My arm was reared back. But what I saw made me bring the baseball back down in front of me. I fingered the seams as I loosely cradled the ball and squinted down the street, trying to make sense of it.

It was Daddy.

I studied his face, as he came closer, coming home early. He didn't look sick. At least he didn't look like he was going to throw up or anything. At the same time, he didn't look happy... but he didn't look mad either. He looked worried. Maybe scared. As he got closer, I could see his eyes were darting around, and a bunch of wrinkles had stacked up and filled his forehead. Wrinkles were even going up and down between his eyebrows.

Carl turned around to see what I was staring at. Daddy breezed by him. As he flew towards the door, he said, "Carl, get home. And when you get home, *stay inside.*"

Carl knew better than to question my daddy. If I was over at their house and Carl's father, Mr. Jenkins, told me to do something, I did it. You didn't argue with *anybody's* parents. Carl didn't argue with Daddy, but he *did* hesitate. It was like my friend was so confused, his feet were frozen in place. His eyes got wide. His mouth fell open just a little.

"*Now*, Carl! Go home."

There was a snap to Daddy's voice, a bite, that I hardly ever heard.

Daddy was a big man. He had muscles in his arms that felt like metal cords when he hugged me. He had a way of walking that made me think of the dinosaur

2

days with those heavy four-legged ones like the stegosaurus. If I was alive in those days, I figured when they put their feet down, step by step, there was a quiet power that made the ground thunder a little. It was the same with Daddy. He walked deliberately but with determination.

I said good-bye to him and watched Carl head down the street. I wondered why Daddy was home so early. But he wasn't having any of that either. I barely got out the beginning of a question before he barked at me to get inside and then called out to Mama.

He had the same sharp edge to his voice with Mama that he'd used with Carl.

Usually, if anybody was thinking about walking across my mother's floor when it was still wet from mopping, she fussed at them up one side and down the other, but just like I stopped when I saw Daddy flying down the street, she stopped fussing before she even started because of the tone in Daddy's voice. She must have heard the same hardness in his voice that I did. When she turned around, she must have seen the same expression on his face that I had seen because she didn't say a word about her floor getting messy again. Daddy told Mama to get Livvie occupied in her room with something. He said I could stay in the kitchen, that he needed to talk to the two of us.

I searched my memory for anything I'd done that was wrong, anything that would make Daddy think we needed to talk, but I couldn't think of a thing.

My daddy paced back and forth, from the door to the sink and back again, over and over, while I waited. When Mama walked back in, Daddy sat down and looked at me across the table from him and at Mama, who was still standing.

Her arms were crossed. It was like she was hugging herself.

"It's all over the *Tulsa Tribune*. Dick Rowland's in trouble. Big trouble."

"Dick Rowland? Isn't he Miss Damie's boy?" Mama said. She pulled at her dress collar with one of her hands. "What kind of trouble is he in?"

"The newspaper says he assaulted a White girl. A colored boy putting his hands on a White girl? Margaret, you know good and well how this is going to end up."

I glanced at Mama. No longer was she embracing herself. Now, her hands were clamped down on her chest, like she was keeping her heart from beating right out of her rib cage.

"What do the White folks want?" Mama sank down into the chair at the end of the table. Her hands slid down out of sight. My eyes went back and forth between the two of them, but it was like Mama had forgotten I was there. Her eyes were glued on Daddy.

"They want the boy dead, Margaret. They want him hanging from a tree, and then they want to tear his body into pieces for souvenirs." He ran his hands along the sides of his face with so much force, his cheeks got stretched out for a moment. Daddy's big, oil-stained hands ended up on top of the table, clasped together. Was he praying?

"James, where is he? Is he on the loose?"

"No, the sheriff's got him."

Phhhuuu. Maybe Mama had been holding her breath because when she let it out, it was like she was letting her worry out with it. "Then he's safe. That's good."

"He ain't safe, Margaret. You know how mobs are. A bunch of White folks, all angry? If they all want the same thing, I don't think the sheriff can stop them, no matter how many guns he has."

Daddy stared at me, but he was talking to Mama. "I think another colored boy is going to lose his life tonight."

22 days ago
Monday, May 9, 1921

Some dogs are all bark, but not my mama—she wasn't ever afraid to bite.

"Henry, I told you. Sweep the walk. Now!" In some families that would have been girls' work. Sweeping. Cooking. Ironing. Livvie would get stuck doing those kinds of chores when she got older, along with doing the dishes and hanging out the wash. Not so in the Simmons family. Mama and Daddy thought of us kids as equal opportunity pack mules. Whatever work there was to do was loaded on our backs, no matter whose back it was. If it was something that even a five-year old could do, Livvie was expected to do it. Otherwise, I had to do it without a smidgen of sass or complaining.

I didn't mind sweeping. Moving around the broom, doing more acting like I was sweeping than actual work, was easy. I got lost inside my head. Mama always thought I had cars on the brain, but mostly, it was baseball and being famous for something that took over my thoughts.

A couple of years earlier when I was ten, Daddy took me and only me to a Monarchs game. Livvie pitched a fit 'cause she wasn't invited. (I think she was only interested in some peanuts to crack open at the game since she didn't know the Monarchs from the Black Crackers.)

Reading about players and seeing their statistics in the newspaper was nothing compared to seeing a real game. I'd heard stories about Dobie Moore, how he could drill a double like it was nothing, how he could send a ball so far with his bat, later it would be found two blocks away.

And Dobie liked the bad balls the best. He'd chop at the high ones and loved the low and outside ones the best. Pitchers sometimes got him out, but they'd have to throw strikes to get him. If they threw him trash balls, he ate 'em up.

The newspaper articles about the Monarch games were just black ink on white paper. Being in the stands and watching them play? That made my insides glow red-hot. For starters, when the players walked out onto the dusty infield, everybody perked up and sat with their backs straighter, like there was electricity in the air. Folks yelled out players' names. Women squealed a little, like they couldn't hold in their excitement any longer.

And when they made an unbelievable play, the stands shook. Everybody got up and stomped and cheered.

I stopped sweeping and leaned on the broom. Just thinking of the thunder from the crowd made me daydream. What if they were shouting *my* name? Henry! Henry! What would that feel like? How would I react if—

What was that? My dream was cut short by something rustling behind me. I grabbed the broom and spun around. It wouldn't surprise me to see that Mama had snuck up on me and was about ready to smack me upside my head for lollygagging. Thankfully, it must have been the breeze blowing some of the bushes around or something else, but it wasn't Mama.

I might not get so lucky the next time. I started moving the broom around more, so if Mama looked out the window or opened the screen door, at least she might think I was working instead of goofing off.

I remembered that day Daddy and I went to a Monarchs game so clearly because I saw Dobie Moore smack a ball that was way outside. The ball hit the ground, bounced back up, and ended up a triple. Folks called him the Black Cat. Sitting in the stands and seeing that play, I understood why. That man was graceful and sneaky as a cat. The people in the stands hooted and hollered when he turned that terrible pitch into a piece of treasure. I dumped my peanuts all over the ground over that one and wasn't even upset. I'd seen a fine athlete at work.

As I swished the broom from side to side, I started sidestepping, as I tried to imagine using grace to avoid getting tagged out by a baseman. Picking my feet up and setting them back down, as I shuffled around with fast, short steps, I glanced back at the house. No sign of Mama.

That afternoon at the ball game, sitting next to Daddy and seeing the living, breathing Rube Currie throw his famous curveballs made me laugh. It was easy for me since I wasn't the one getting humiliated in front of a bunch of people by a ball of leather and string. The Buckeye players made little clouds of dust rise up, as they dug in their shoes and positioned their bats in the sweetest place possible, but it did no good. Currie's balls went wide and curved in with such fierceness, they were impossible to hit. The batters saw the ball zoom past them and shook their heads in wonderment.

What if all it took for people to shout out my name and squeal over me was if I walked onto a baseball field? How would that feel to know I had the power to entertain and amaze people?

As I swept, I imagined I was one of the Monarchs and the game was tied in the ninth inning. I was pretty sure Mama wasn't watching me through the window, so I put the broom handle on my shoulder and brought it around in a mighty swing to make a game-winning homerun. And when I hung up laundry, I pretended one of the clothespins was a baseball; and I turned it over in my hand, as I imagined how pitchers turned the balls over in their hands, how the seams felt in their fingers, how they might have had a lucky spot on the balls, as they positioned them snug in their palms.

Some voices down the block made my daydream disappear. I started sweeping in earnest. I might have fooled Mama when she was still in the house, but once she came out to greet the voices and saw our section of the street not looking good, she would have my rear end not looking good.

The screen door banged. Mama yelled. The edge in her voice made me jump. "Henry. Get sweeping. You should have been done a long time ago."

More dreams about being as famous as Dobie Moore had to wait until later. The one good thing about going to bed at night? I could let my thoughts drift to wherever I wanted them to without being worried about Mama snarling about me being too slow at hanging up the laundry or any other chore 'cause even Mama couldn't intrude on my dreams.

.

Tuesday, May 10, 1921

I saw Dick Rowland, and I had some questions for him. I wasn't shy. "Hey Dick! How ya doin'?" There I was, acting like I *knew* him, like we were great friends.

"I'm okay. Can't complain 'cause if I did, who'd listen?" The toothpick danced between his lips.

Dick Rowland was nineteen, so he was too old to want to hang around with kids my age, but I'd heard some of my older cousins talk about him. When he was still at Booker T. Washington High School, he played basketball and football. Dick was tall—just a couple inches shy of six feet back when he was a sophomore—and he was solid as a rock.

There had been a couple of different stories about Dick. Some folks claimed he dropped out of high school and tried to go back and finish but couldn't. Some said he dropped out, so he could earn his own money, and he was, too. Dick was a shoeshiner who worked in White Tulsa, which was not near as safe as Greenwood.

Leaving school to make some money? I liked that idea fine, but I knew better than to even talk about doing that later on down the road. Mama and Daddy would tan my behind if I told them I planned on quitting school when I was a teenager, so I could get a job. Both of them had told me too many times to count, "White folks can take away our rights; they can take away our freedom, but they can't take away our knowledge."

Since Dick was leaning against the bus stop sign, I figured he might not have minded chewing the fat with a kid—only until his bus came along, of course. I had a few minutes to talk while I waited to pick up Livvie from a birthday party.

Did Mama know exactly how long it took to walk from our house to the Monroes' house and back home again? I hoped not.

"Kid, ain't you Ingram's little cousin? Your name Harrison or somethin' like that?"

"Henry. Yeah. I don't get to see Ingram too often, but I know you guys played together on the basketball team."

"Yeah, Henry, those were the glory days, alright. I feel like an old man already, and I ain't even twenty."

"You work at a shoeshine stand, right?"

Dick barely nodded, but I caught it.

"What's that job like? Is it hard?"

"Hard? Naw. It's nothing to make the sweat drip off you, but it makes your insides cry." Dick put his hands in his pockets. "Your pride leaks out at ten cents a pop."

This guy, talking about crying? My daddy never cried—at least I'd never witnessed it—but he was a lot older than Dick. It made me stop and wonder if I should put away any thoughts of shining shoes as a part-time job.

But the lure of money made my brain tumble forward anyway. I knew I couldn't work during the week. Neither Mama nor Daddy would have cottoned to me working and letting my schoolwork suffer. The weekends weren't even a sure thing. But shining shoes was at least work I was capable of doing. "I was thinking of working, shining shoes, on the weekends to earn some spending money. How much do you make?"

Dick's lip curled up. "It ain't what you make that's important. It's what you lose that counts. Kid, you gotta act like a fool to make it as a shiner. In the beginning, when I first started out, I'd stand there next to my shoeshine stand, a chip on my shoulder the size of an elephant, lookin' angry. 'Cause I was. I was mad." Dick shook a fist in the air a few times. "What self-respectin' man wants to be cleaning the mud and the grime and the dog poop off another man's shoes? I mean, there I am every day, at his feet, as low as low can be, and there the White man is, high above me, like he's on a throne."

I backed away from Dick a little and bowed down my head. This was hard to even listen to.

"So in the beginning, when I wasn't making no money, I started watching the other shoeshine boys to see how they did it. Each one of 'em had their own act. Some of 'em sang songs. Some of 'em danced. Some scratched their head like they weren't even capable of a thought. And the stupider they acted, the bigger their tips.

"I made up my own little routine. I do a lot of snappin' and poppin' with my rag. I get real thorough

15

with each step, acting like if I don't do a good job on their filthy shoes, the whole country'll fall apart. Man, I even get a toothbrush out at the end, so I can get every nook and cranny. I try not to talk at all. I'm scared my voice will let them know exactly what I'm thinkin'.'"

Dick shoved me back a little with his fists. "Come on, kid. You don't want no job like that."

I stepped back and nodded.

After hearing what Dick's job was like, I had to agree. It didn't seem like the kind of work I wanted.

The bus gliding up to the stop was a welcome sight since the two of us had fallen into silence. There was something awful about a guy talking about how he was being treated like a dog, and there was nothing he could do about it. He even had to act like he liked being mistreated like that.

Once the bus pulled away, I walked towards Lucille's house. Lucille and Livvie had been best friends since the time they learned to walk. Eventually, they were going to be in first grade together, a little more than a year away, when they were both six, and those two girls were thick as thieves. They didn't get to see much of each other in the evenings or the weekends—little-girl chores and playing with her dolls kept Livvie busy. Birthdays were usually just for the family in Greenwood, except for the milestone ones like the 90th or 100th, but I guess Mr. and Mrs. Monroe thought of Livvie as Lucille's twin sister. I sure wished they were right. Having no sister would surely make my life simpler.

Stepping onto their porch, I knocked. From somewhere in the house, the sound of girlie yelling and laughter drifted toward me. Why did girls giggle so much?

Mrs. Monroe came to the door, wiping her hands on her apron. "Henry, it's so good of you to pick up your sister. You're a good big brother to Olivia. Your parents must be proud of you." She adjusted the scarf that was wound around her head, then tucked in a runaway curl.

Mrs. Monroe must have been in the middle of cooking supper. The smell of onions and browned meat clung to her and teased me. My stomach grumbled, loud enough for her to hear.

"Henry, we have plenty of cake left. Way too much for our family to eat. Would you like some?" Her eyes, golden-brown with flecks of cinnamon, scrunched up with her smile. Leave it to the kind folks of Greenwood to help out a hungry boy.

"Yes, ma'am." Always ma'am and always sir was the way I was taught. Treat folks in a kind way, and I'd get kindness in return. At least it was that way in Greenwood. But in the White part of Tulsa, no matter how much kindness and good manners we doled out, all we got back was meanness.

Why was it like that? Why did White folks look at me with hatred in their eyes, just because of the color I was? If we went deeper than our skin, weren't we all the same? God made all mankind from the same mold, right?

I'd asked Mama and Daddy about it. Sometimes they gave me answers just to shush me up.

"That's the way it's always been. Now get back to your chores."

"I don't know. Some folks just don't know how to treat other folks. Now start doin' your homework."

"Son, this kind of treatment has been hundreds of years in the making. We can't stop it. We can't change it. We just got to deal with it."

But sometimes, we got into a deep discussion, a history lesson of sorts. Mostly from Daddy (and from Mama when I could get her to sit still long enough). In those talks, I'd learned that a while back, the Frisco railroad tracks divided Tulsa into two sections: the White section and our section. It's not like we wanted to be separate from White folks. It just happened. And that's the way it still was.

Back then, Greenwood was called "Little Africa," and through lots of sweat and scrimping and saving, the people in Greenwood worked hard and built our town. Brick buildings sprang up along Greenwood Avenue. Night clubs, theaters, churches, banks. We had two newspapers, more than 10,000 people, and some of us had indoor plumbing—something that a lot of White folks didn't even have.

Daddy said we did so good here because we kept our money inside Greenwood. Of course, we didn't have much choice. Business folks bragged that every dollar bill around here got passed around 50-60 times before it left Greenwood, and that said something. Mama said we liked to honor the businesses in our neighborhood by spending our money at Greenwood shops. It also sort of said that White people weren't always excited about doing business with us, so we had to keep passing around the same money to other colored folks.

From the bits I'd pieced together, it seemed like the better off we got, the madder some White folks got. Mama and Daddy heard muttering and insults from White people whenever they had to venture out of

Greenwood. There were stories in the *Tulsa Star* and the *Oklahoma Sun* about KKK activities in Oklahoma, and just last week, there was an article about folks about the age of Mama and Daddy who got fined $10 just because they refused to sit at the back of a streetcar. Even me, not even close to grown-up, could see what was going on.

It was too bad. It was too bad that the kindness I showed Mrs. Monroe and the kindness she gave back to me wasn't the way it was everywhere. By way, the cake was delicious. White cake with dark chocolate icing. The piece I got was a corner—my favorite.

Thursday, May 12, 1921

Mama gave me some usual orders. "Henry, keep an eye on Olivia. I've got these cupboards to scrub out. You hear me?"

"Oh Mama, do I have to? I was about to—"

Mama cut her eyes at me so sharply, I thought she might have drawn blood. I didn't say another word. "Yes, Mama." Because it was too pretty of an afternoon to get stuck inside the house, and since I was not eager to be subjected to Mama's hawk-like watch, I decided I'd watch Livvie outside.

"Livvie, let's go." I grabbed her hand and guided her outside. She didn't really have to be dragged around when I wanted her to do something. If she thought there was a chance I'd play with her, she followed me like a puppy dog.

Livvie tugged on my hand. "Henry, let's play house. You can be the daddy, and I can be the mama. We can make our house over there." She pointed to the spot between the rose bushes.

My eyes rolled. I couldn't help it. Oh Lord. I'd done this too many times, so I had to squirm out of it somehow. "Not now, Livvie. You go set up your house. Maybe I'll play with you later." I hoped that when later rolled around, she had forgotten.

Little four-year old Wess Young, a chubby-legged, big-cheeked boy, saved the day.

Livvie had me halfway across the yard when I spied Wess, walking along with his mother.

"Mrs. Young, good mornin'. It's a beautiful day, isn't it?"

"It is, Henry," she said as Wess shuffled his feet back and forth and kicked the rocks around. His mother kept adjusting her grip on his hand. But he twisted around like a snake in a bag.

"Wess sure is a busy boy. Where are the two of you headed, ma'am?"

Thank the Lord Livvie never squirmed like that. Wess was half wild animal, half kid. But his busy-body ways came in handy today.

"Oh, we're going to get some groceries at Mann's if I can manage to keep up with this child." She smiled proudly down at her son but exhaled loudly out of her nose. I recognized that noise. I did the same when I was so aggravated with Livvie, my nerves got frayed.

"Mrs. Young, would you like to leave Wess here while you shop? Would you mind? Wess and Livvie could play together. I promise to keep an eye on them." I'd keep my eyes glued on them, but with the two of them corralled in the yard, I wasn't going to have to play a blessed lick with either one of them.

I raised my eyebrows expectantly towards Mrs. Young, making it seem like I was the most charitable boy in the world, like it was a selfless act I was about to perform. Sometimes, I was a wonderful actor.

Her eyes widened. "Would I mind? Certainly not. You'd be doing me a great favor, Henry. But are you sure? Two children? Two active children? You sure it wouldn't be too much for you to handle?" She ran her hand across the top of Wess's head, smoothing down his hair. The other hand continued to hold him firmly next to her or as close to her as she could manage.

"No ma'am, I wouldn't mind, and the two of them wouldn't be too much to handle. But, if I get into a pickle, I'll just holler for my mama. She's inside right now, doing some spring cleaning."

I looked behind me. Livvie was so engrossed in setting up our imaginary house, she was singing to herself, paying no attention to the three of us. She'd rearranged some of the rocks around the roses, which made Mama tsk-tsk every time she had to mound them back up.

"A place for everything, and everything in its place," Mama would say.

I couldn't figure out why it was so all-fired important that there was a special arrangement for the rocks, but I knew better than to question Mama.

"Livvie, come here." She stood still as a statue, a rock in her hand, and stared at us. "Come on, Livvie. Hurry up."

She dropped her rock and trotted over. Livvie and Wess eyed each other, like they were dogs sizing each other up.

"Wess, if your mama says it's okay, you and Livvie are gonna get to play together while your mama gets her shopping done. Is that fine with you, Mrs. Young?"

A look of relief washed across her face. I sometimes saw my mama all frazzled after going on a shopping excursion with Livvie in tow.

"It's fine with me as long as Wess promises to be on his best behavior. Wess, you'd best behave, you hear me?"

The boy nodded. I knew it might be a different story once his mama was halfway down the block and out of earshot, but for right now, he pledged to be a model young citizen.

"I owe you a heap of gratitude, Henry. I shouldn't be too long. I just need a few things, and I'll be able to get the list taken care of quicker without my helper." She winked at me.

"Take your time, Mrs. Young. These two will have fun. There's no need to hurry back. They'll be fine, just fine." *And so will I*, I thought to myself. I'd be fine, just sitting off to the side and making sure they didn't get hurt while they were on my watch.

And I wouldn't have to hold no baby dolls or give my little sister a kiss on the cheek when I came home from "work" or sat down to a pretend supper.

Either Wess would do all that, or they'd sort themselves out and play a different game. It wasn't my problem no more!

I lucked out. Livvie and Wess played together for a little more than an hour. And I sat there and acted like I was keeping a close eye on them because really, I watched them just enough to make sure neither one of them got hurt. And Mama was none the wiser.

For dinner, we had black-eyed peas and fresh yeast rolls. Like always, Daddy filled his plate first. I watched him as he buttered his roll. There was always a thin line of motor oil and grime under his fingernails and in the cuts in his hands—grime that no soap and water could reach.

One time, when Livvie was getting ready for church, she noticed Daddy's fingernails and commented on them. "Daddy, you forgot to wash your hands." My father looked down, thinking part of his breakfast had dripped onto a hand, saw nothing but the always-there grease, and gave Liv a little lesson.

"Olivia, life is sometimes dirty. Makin' a living sometimes involves dirty work. And just livin' today is often times dirty and nasty for colored folks. But it can't be helped. We just keep movin' forward, doing our best and giving thanks for another day."

Some families just shoveled the food in at mealtime, too busy chewing and swallowing to talk. Not so at the Simmonses' dinner table. Breakfast was eaten in a hurry during the week. I had to rush my morning meal, so I could hightail it to school. Daddy was in a hurry to get to work. Mama was always in a rush, so she could get "her boys" out of her hair, and she and Livvie could begin their routine of house chores. Dinner was different.

At dinner time, we all had important news we shared—at least that's what Daddy and Mama thought. Things happened during the day to all of us—newsworthy events—and my parents paid as close attention to the talk that took place at the supper table as they did to the front-page stories in the newspaper.

"What did you do at school today, Henry?" Daddy's eyebrows arched up in anticipation.

My daddy would probably slap the side of my head if I said, "Nothin'." For me (and next year for Livvie), schoolwork was like the repair work he did at the automobile shop. "Do it honestly. Take pride in it. Do it well, and when you make a mistake, you learn from it." At least that's what my parents tried to pound into my head.

Livvie chimed in. "Well, I know one thing Henry did. Henry ripped his school pants because when he got home, I saw—Ow!"

I had slid down a little in my chair and kicked my sister. Kicked her a good one.

Her eyes opened wide in surprise. What did she expect, tattling on me like that?

Mama was too distracted by a new mending job she'd have to work on later tonight to pay any attention to Livvie. "Henry, do I need to sew up your pants?"

"I'm sorry, Mama. We were playing ball in the school yard. I was running after what ended up being a homerun, and when I was almost..." I let my voice fade away when I saw she had her hand up. My mother no more wanted to listen to me talk about sports than I wanted to play dollies with my sister. At that moment, all she cared about was getting the mending done, so I would have school clothes to wear.

"Just be sure to put them in the mending basket when you get ready for bed tonight," and she ate another spoonful of black-eyed peas.

Livvie glanced at me and then at Mama. "Mama, Henry just—" I slid down again, stretched out my leg and barely tapped her leg. My eyebrow raised up, telling her that was just a reminder. If she insisted on tattling on me again, I'd follow through with another full-fledged kick.

Then I smiled.

Livvie got the message and quieted down.

"We're all working on writing history reports," I said. "Miss Marion said my report has promise so far. Today, she taught us about a man named Edward McCabe. Did you know he was interested in getting a whole state of colored people?"

"What did you say? Repeat that, please," Mama said. It sounded like she didn't believe me. Although the story about Mr. McCabe wasn't in our history books, Miss Marion was a history buff. She wouldn't have made up a story, and she wasn't ever wrong. My teacher was always reading about something historical while we ate our lunch. She had a way of making the past come alive.

"Yeah, he was a colored man who wanted lots of colored people to migrate to Oklahoma. I think Miss Marion said Mr. McCabe wanted the state to be a 'majority Black state' because in the South colored folks' freedom was denied, and their dreams were being squashed."

Mama nodded her head while I talked. Daddy muttered under his breath, just loud enough for Mama and me but too quiet for Livvie to even catch his drift. "I know what it's like to be squashed."

Mama cut her eyes at him and told him, *That's enough,* with just a glance.

"Is that so, son?" Daddy said as he looked at Mama with a playful twinkle in his eyes. Just like he'd buttered up his roll a few minutes earlier, now he started buttering up Mama.

"I guess he was good at convincing people because between 1900 and 1906, the number of Black people in Oklahoma doubled. Edward McCabe claimed that the Oklahoma territory was... How did he put it?" I searched back into my mind as I tried to remember what our teacher had told us. "Oh, now I remember. McCabe said Oklahoma was 'the paradise of Eden and the garden of the gods.' "

"Too bad he'd forgotten that White devils were part of the equation," and this time it was Mama who mumbled under her breath. What she said tickled her so, she actually snorted. My daddy looked like his wife had committed a crime. He looked at Mama in mock horror, his eyes bugged out and his mouth hung open in pretend shock.

"Miss Marion said lots more about lynchings. She said—"

But my voice couldn't go on any further. I shoved a piece of cornbread into my mouth and chewed til it was way past mush. It was too horrible to believe. My teacher told us White folks would have a party when they had a hanging. Staring at my black-eyed peas, I stirred them around on my plate. Recalling when my teacher described some of the "fun" they had— sometimes they'd even tear off hunks of whoever got hanged, to show off to others—I shuddered a little. From the way Miss Marion put it, they sounded like wild dogs that had been caged-up and starved for a couple of weeks, not people. Did people *really* do things like that?

I looked up. I looked up from my plate at Mama and Daddy. Maybe I had stopped talking only a second ago, but it seemed like a lot longer. My parents were listening. Waiting for me to finish what I was working on saying.

Mama said, "Henry? Go on. What else did your teacher tell you?"

I took a deep breath. I bowed down my head, looking just at the food still left on my plate. To talk about something that bad, it was all I could do to say the words. To see my parents looking at me at the same time? I didn't think I could do it. What if it was a story Miss Marion told us to make us pay attention? Worse, what if it were true?

"Son, what did you learn? Tell us." Daddy's deep voice pressed me on.

"Miss Marion said that more and more Black faces made the White people nervous. They used—and still do—lynchings to keep Black folks afraid. She said the White ladies would stand with their parasols, so they wouldn't get too hot, the men would smoke and laugh, and the young ones would play as they watched people get hanged. My teacher even said they'd make postcards of Black boys dangling from a tree, so they'd have a souvenir. Is that really true?" I looked at both my parents, hoping they'd tell me Miss Marion had been pulling my leg, that she had been adding made-up details to make it more interesting for us.

My daddy glanced at Mama and then said, "I've seen a couple of those postcards in Tulsa store windows on display. I steer clear of stores that cater to that kind of customer...and I'm sure they appreciate me doing that." Daddy smiled a half-sad smile.

Straightening up so her spine was like a broomstick, Mama changed the subject. "Olivia, why don't you tell your daddy what you did today?" She cocked her head and gave Daddy another look. Her eyes squinched til they were almost shut, and her mouth pursed up. I could read the message Mama was sending just as well as Daddy.

Livvie stirred her food around on her plate. Then she put a spoonful of the black-eyed peas in her mouth. She chewed and swallowed before she answered.

"Mama showed me how to roll the dough to make cloverleaf rolls. And I worked on writing my name—first and last. Mama said my i's are pretty as a picture."

As he held up a piece of his roll, Daddy said, "That's nice, baby. These are mighty tasty rolls, and as far as your handwriting, folks get judged by their penmanship. Well-formed words mean the person is higher-quality, from some people's way of thinking."

"It's a shame you don't practice what you preach, James Henry Simmons. Your writing is a sloppy mess," Mama said.

Everybody laughed. Livvie a little behind the rest of us since she probably didn't figure out it was a joke until everyone else was chuckling. My daddy's handwriting was like a foreign language. Put a pen or pencil in his hand, and only he could read what ended up on the paper. But put a broken-down carburetor into his calloused hands, and he could work magic.

Mama talked about the things she'd gotten done around the house. Daddy talked about the two cars he worked on at the shop. One he finished fixing and one he'd have to keep working on tomorrow.

Once our plates were scraped clean with bits of bread and spoons, Livvie cleared the table (with me right next to her, to make sure she didn't break anything), and then I washed the dishes. Mama went into the front room to do some mending. Her mending basket was bottomless, what with Daddy regularly getting small rips in his shirt and pants from sharp car parts, and Livvie constantly tripping and then falling because she was always looking where she'd been instead of where she was going. And socks. To keep a family in socks, Mama said, took a whole lot of darning. When our toes peeked out or when the heel got a hole, Mama darned the sock up til it was almost like new.

That night as I lay in bed, I thought about Daddy's remark. White folks were squashing us. They were keeping us down. Colored folks were working hard but not getting ahead. It's like we were treading water, and the only thing sticking out of the water was our nose.

Not being able to look around, not being able to hold our head up high in some places—that was no way to live.

Sunday, May 22, 1921

Sunday mornings were always a rush, as we all hurried to eat breakfast and get into our best clothes. As usual, Mama inspected me and Livvie before we left the house. She had to put a bit more grease on my sister's face and readjusted some of her stray hairs. For once, I passed inspection with flying colors the first time.

Or at least I was flying as high as a twelve-year-old boy could. I'd never look perfect. I was a boy. Mama would never look at me dressed for church and be as happy as she was when she saw Livvie all gussied up in her smocked and lacy dresses and her patent leather shoes and her hair bows dancing at the end of her short braids. No, a boy dressed up was different, but I'd learned what Mama looked for. Hair smoothed down. Clothes clean and brushed off. Shoes polished and shined. Face clean with a slight sheen. I liked to rub in the grease on my own face. When Mama did it or when she licked her finger and wiped a smudge of something off my face, I felt like I was Livvie's age all over again. So on Sundays or when I knew Mama was going to be extra particular about my appearance, I'd take a dab of the petroleum jelly and rub it onto my face all over. If Mama even saw a small patch of ashy skin, she'd swoop down, and when she did it, she wasn't always gentle. Whenever she'd get done, I felt like a pile of bread dough. The skin on my face had been kneaded and moved around so much, I only hoped she hadn't put my nose or a cheek in the wrong spot.

After we all passed inspection, even Daddy, we headed to church.

About midway through the service, when Mama got up in front of the whole congregation and sang her solo, her song surprised me. I didn't know about Livvie or Daddy. Maybe Livvie had heard her practice during the day when the rest of us were gone, or maybe Mama rehearsed in front of Daddy late at night, after I'd fallen asleep.

I figured she was singing, "Gonna Lay Down My Burden." That was one of her favorites. When she started to sing a different song, and nothing but her voice filled the church—no piano to accompany her— my mouth dropped open. All I could do was listen. Once she sang the first line, it was like the whole congregation froze up, like Mama was the only one in a canyon of silence, and she was trying her best to get her voice to bounce off the cliff sides and shatter the granite—until there was nothing left but a pile of rocks.

No more auction block for me.
No more, no more.
No more auction block for me.
Many thousand gone.

No more peck of corn for me.
No more, no more.
No more peck of corn for me.
Many thousand gone.

No more driver's lash for me.
No more, no more.
No more driver's lash for me.
Many thousand gone.

No more pint of salt for me.
No more, no more.
No more pint of salt for me.
Many thousand gone.

No more hundred lash for me.
No more, no more.
No more hundred lash for me.
Many thousand gone.

No more mistress call for me.
No more, no more.
No more mistress call for me.
Many thousand gone.

No more children stole from me.
No more, no more.
No more children stole from me.
Many thousand gone.

No more slavery chains for me.
No more, no more.
No more slavery chains for me.
Many thousand gone.

Usually when a solo would finish, there'd be some "amens" and some "hallelujahs" in response. This time was different. This time, when Mama finished the last line and bowed her head, the rest of the church, without it planned or talked about, sang the last verse again, like they were joining in on Mama's demands.

After that, Mama walked back to our pew, her head still down.

As we walked home, no one said anything about Mama's song. We talked about the preacher and how long-winded he was. We talked about Mrs. Meacher's hat. Daddy and I thought it made her look like a peacock, but Mama did her best to shush our laughter. We talked about how pretty the wildflowers were at the pulpit. But we tiptoed around the song Mama had decided to sing.

Sunday afternoons were the opposite of Sunday mornings. In the afternoon, we had supper and were expected to read. At least I was expected to do that, and Livvie looked at pictures in books. Daddy usually read the paper and napped in his chair. It was against Mama's nature to just sit and do anything as still and as unproductive as reading, so she usually busied herself with some stitching that was just for her. No darning. No mending, but instead, some embroidery work to pretty up the house. To her, that wasn't work. That was joy.

It was the Lord's day, Mama and Daddy reminded us on a regular basis. Even God made our world and took a day to rest.

I lay on the floor reading, sprawled between the couch and Daddy's chair. Mama's solo swirled around in my head. It was an angry song, but it was a quiet, smoldering fury kind of anger. Like Mama was holding her hand, all balled-up, in the pocket of her dress, and she was ready to hit someone with that fist of hers. This wasn't the Mama I knew. I figured I didn't have much to lose if I asked her respectfully about it.

I turned my book over to save my spot, sat up, and said, "Mama. Your song today..." My voice trailed off, my vocal cords losing courage fast. I had no idea what I should say next that would not get Mama mad at me.

"Yes?" she said idly and didn't even look up from the needle and embroidery floss gliding in and out of the tea-colored cotton fabric. Mama had little time for anything that involved artistry, so she savored it when it fell into her lap.

"The song you sang today. It's not the kind of song you usually choose to sing." I figured I'd ease into it.

Mama anchored the needle into the fabric and looked at me. Her eyes widened. I sat up a bit straighter. I glanced over at Livvie, playing with her doll on the floor between the couch and the front door. She stopped fussing with her baby doll, her eyes darting back and forth between Mama and me. Livvie always nosed into things when she thought I might get in trouble. Somehow, she must have been able to tell I was nervous, and now she was happy to watch whatever was going to happen.

"What made you pick that song?" My spine was straight, but my courage was crumpling fast.

Questioning Mama about what she did wasn't something I did very often.

"'Many Thousand Gone' is a song that's been around for ages. It used to be popular in the 1800s. Why do you ask, Henry?" Now not only were Mama's eyes wide open, but her eyebrows were perked up as well.

"It just didn't seem like the kind of song you usually sing in church." I didn't add what else I was thinking, *It sounded like you were lashing out with your voice, like you were mad as a wet cat, and everyone sitting in that congregation was in danger of getting cut with your voice.* I gathered my gumption up. If I didn't try to get an answer from her now, I'd always be curious. I'd always regret it, and I'd never ever know. "Mama, it almost seemed like you picked that song because of something you're feeling deep down inside."

"Henry, aren't you supposed to be reading?" Livvie's eyes were now round as baseballs, her way of pretending she was an innocent angel, an angel only intent on doing good. One way or another, my sister was determined I would get in trouble.

"Livvie, it's okay for Henry—or you—to ask questions. I don't want you to ever think anything different. And Henry, I *am* feeling something deep in the core of my heart. It's a feeling I was born with. It's a feeling my mama and daddy were born with, too. They didn't want to pass it on to me, but they didn't have a choice." She set her embroidery onto the side table.

"Baby, the feeling I'm trying to keep from exploding out of me is rage. I know I keep harping on you and your sister, telling you two to keep control of yourselves, and that's right. It is the right thing to do—

most of the time. But sometimes—" Mama blew out a big, noisy breath, so loud, it even woke up Daddy from his nap. "Sometimes, I can hardly help myself. Even a good-natured dog can only get beat so many times before he growls and bites."

Mama gestured at Daddy. "Look at your father. He's a proud man. A strong man. A hard-workin' man. But when he gets called 'boy' by White people, he knows if he loses his temper and sets them straight, he'll be goin' to jail."

Mama leaned forward and continued, "Henry, I want you to grow up in a world where if you do an equal amount of work, you'll get an equal amount of pay. I wish with all my heart that when you get to be big and strong like your daddy, you'll be called a 'man' instead of 'boy' by everyone you encounter. And I pray that soon, this hatred over Black and White comes to an end—forever."

"Margaret, you want some sweet tea?" Daddy got up and headed towards the kitchen.

"Not right now, James, but thank you." She shifted to glance in my daddy's direction and then turned back to me. "Henry, you're gonna have to find a way to let your anger out. For me, it's singing. I let my voice soar to heights I'm never gonna reach, and I let my voice go so low and sad, I feel like I'm in the bottom of a freshly dug grave. For your daddy, believe it or not, it's work. Your daddy can beat on those car parts with a hammer or swing a wrench at 'em and get lots of mad right out of his system. For you, it might be sports. Or maybe, it will be writing." Mama picked up her sewing and pulled the needle out of the cotton. "So yes, Henry. There was a reason why I chose 'Many Thousand Gone.' It's a song I needed to sing. It's a song that needed to be sung. Maybe it's a song you needed to hear."

That night as I stretched out in bed, the lines from the song swirled around in my head, wrapped themselves around my heart, and squeezed. No more hundred lashes. No more children stole from their mamas and daddies. No more chains.

When would the lashes that White folks gave us with their voices come to an end? When would the chains of White people's laws come to an end?

When would there be no more hate?

Tuesday, May 31, 1921, 4:00 p.m.

I wanted to play some ball with Carl. The two of us had a running competition going on. We'd see who could throw the most stinger balls—pitches that were thrown so hard and so fast, they made the catcher's hand hurt, even through the glove.

That's all I wanted, but the afternoon didn't go the way I'd planned. Not at all.

Before our ball playing got interrupted from Daddy coming home early, I had done what I needed to do to get outside. Since schoolwork came first at my house, I finished my homework lickety-split. It was too perfect outside to lollygag in the house, too little time left before dinner to waste time daydreaming in-between math problems. It was warm, but not make-you-drip-with-sweat hot yet. The sky was pure blue without a cloud in sight. In other words, it was an afternoon made for goofing off.

Carl and I were in the front yard. I think I was ahead as far as stingers, but we slipped in curve balls and changeups along with our fast balls.

When I saw Daddy coming down the street in a hurry, I held onto the baseball and just stared, trying to figure out why he was coming home so early. Carl turned around, curious to see what I was looking at.

I wanted to ask him, "Daddy, what're you doing here this time of the afternoon? You sick?" But I didn't. He didn't look sick, but he also didn't look like he felt okay either. Sweat dripped down his face and had worked its way down the front of his shirt. His eyes had that worried look about them, like they got when he and Mama sat at the table and worked on paying the bills. His lips were thinned into a hard line.

"Carl, get home. And when you get home, *stay inside.*" There was a steely sound to Daddy's voice. "Now, Carl! Go home." His words came out like pieces of metal. Hard. Unbending.

Carl glanced at Daddy and then at me with a questioning look on his face, but he knew better. My daddy, just like Carl's daddy or any of our daddies, wasn't to be messed with. Sometimes they played ball with us, and sometimes they wrestled with us. But when our daddies got serious about something, we did what we were told, and we hopped to it.

"See you later, Carl," I said as he turned and headed home.

Carl didn't run, but he moved faster than a walk. I watched as he got smaller and smaller down the block.

Daddy was already at the screen door and held it open. "Get in the house, Henry. Didn't you hear me tellin' Carl to get home and get inside? You too, boy."

"What's wrong, Daddy?" I thought about saying that; I started to say it, but I changed my mind instead, so I just walked across the stoop towards the door.

"Margaret," he called as he walked into the kitchen. Mama was mopping the floor.

Mama turned around to get another patch of tile mopped, but she heard Daddy's voice that sounded like metal, and then she got an eyeful of Daddy. Standing behind him, I couldn't see Daddy, but I saw the look on Mama's face. I'd never seen that expression on Mama. She looked like she was looking at a ghost, like whatever she saw on Daddy's face petrified her.

"What is it, James?" She held the mop up straight, like she needed it to keep herself upright.

"Margaret, get Olivia busy on something in her bedroom and then come back here. Henry can stay here. He needs to hear what I got to say," Daddy sat down at the kitchen table. Mama's messed-up floor was no longer important, I figured. The mop got propped up in the corner, a silent reminder.

It was then that Daddy told us about Dick Rowland, that White folks were thinking he had done something to a White girl, and now they wanted to lynch him.

My bladder almost let loose when I heard the word lynching. From what I'd been learning at school, all over the South, colored boys and colored men were getting hanged so much, they were like peaches dangling from the trees. But a lynching here? In Greenwood? I chewed on my lip. The rusty taste of blood washed over my taste buds while my mind tried to make sense of things. I'd just seen Dick at the bus stop a few weeks ago. And now there were people wanting to kill him?

I peeked at Mama to see how she was taking the news. Mama sat down and just stared at Daddy, not even blinking, like she didn't want to miss anything that passed across Daddy's face.

"What do they say the boy did?" She was part terrified and part curious. So was I.

"The White folks claim it's something serious, but most of the colored folks think it was just an accident. Apparently, Dick was in an elevator with the White elevator girl, name of Sarah Page. She screamed. White folks jumped right on it and called it assault. Colored people who know more about it than I do say it was probably just the boy stumbling and having to catch his balance, and he touched her accidentally. You know, how the elevator sometimes comes to a jerky stop? Anyway, Dick Rowland ran, and not too much later, the sheriff and his boys got him."

"James! If the police have him, isn't he safe in a jail cell?"

"You know as well as I do, Margaret. A mob of angry people? They're as powerful as floodwater."

When Daddy said that, in my mind, I saw a swollen river rushing along, carrying all sorts of stuff, as the flood broke up things in its path. Could a mob be that destructive and bent on breaking up another human?

"I don't know if any one person would be safe up against a mob, sweetie," Daddy said. "I just know we need to lay low, stay buttoned up in the house, and hope that trouble doesn't find us."

Hunched over, Mama cradled her face in her hands, using her fingers to hide her eyes. When she sat back up, she said, "No need to go out of our way to find problems. Let's take on the trouble when it comes knocking on our door, and not a minute before." She scooted back her chair and got up. "And now, if you all would kindly get off my kitchen floor, so I can mop it again, I'd appreciate it." There was frustration in my mama's voice, like we'd gotten on her nerves.

Things got back to normal. Livvie came out of her room, showing off her coloring. Daddy sang some silly songs (I thought he made them up) that caused Livvie to laugh. Mama finished mopping and then made dinner. That night we had ham and beans and cornbread. On nights when we had cornbread, Daddy would crumble up a piece in a glass, then he'd pour milk over it. He said it was like dessert. I tried it once. I sure didn't agree.

We were quiet after eating. I heard Livvie humming to herself, like she did most evenings. I felt safe.

I was safe because I had Mama and Daddy looking out for me.

Tuesday, May 31, 1921, 6:10 p.m.

When the phone rang, Daddy answered it. I was reading; Livvie was playing with one of her dolls behind the couch. Although I tried to hear what he said to whoever called, Daddy kept his voice too low for me to catch onto the conversation.

When he hung up, he said something—deep and quiet again—to Mama. Whatever he said to her made her upset enough that she spoke loud enough for me and Livvie to hear. "What do you think the White folks are planning on doin'? Gettin' the sheriff to okay a lynching? Sheriff McCullough's White, but I don't think he'd do a foolish thing like that. Do you?"

I'd heard Mama ask me questions like that before. *I don't think that room is clean. Do you? I don't think that's a very good grade. Do you? I don't think you look even close to presentable. Do you?* I could also guess the look she shot at Daddy 'cause I got those looks all the time.

I was on the couch, but I needed to get closer, so I could hear everything. I stretched out on the floor on the edge of the rug closest to the kitchen. Something was going on. My mind returned to when Dick and I had talked earlier in the month, while he was waiting for the bus. At that moment, his big problem was having to swallow his pride, so he could get tips as a shoeshiner. Now? Now, he was in jail. Did he know what trouble was brewing with the White folks? I didn't know, but I was pretty sure he did know how serious it was to get accused of doing something bad to a White person...especially a White girl.

I heard Daddy get up—at least I figured it was Daddy since I could hear his boots hit the tile with each step—and then the sound of running water. "I don't know," he said. "I can't say what a bunch of White folks, all in a lather, will do. Ed said some of the preachers and shop owners are wanting to organize a group. They think Dick Rowland is going to need some protection." I heard a newspaper shake like it was being opened. Daddy went on. "From this editorial, I'd say they're right."

"James, there'll be preachers and shop owners. The sheriff and his deputies too, right?" From what I could hear, it sounded like Mama was begging Daddy to make her feel better. She continued, "The White folks bend the laws, I know that, but are they gonna break them right in front of a sheriff?" A chair moved. "I'm gonna check on the children," and before I could roll away from the kitchen, Mama was on top of me, and she was staring me down.

"What are you up to?" she said. Her nostrils flared, and she knew. She knew what my big nose and my big ears were up to. No reason to have tried to come up with a lie, so I just looked away and tried not to look too guilty.

Mama glanced at Livvie, then went back into the kitchen and whispered something to Daddy.

"Henry, come in here," he said quietly.

I got up and shuffled the couple of steps into the kitchen.

"Yes, sir?"

"Earlier today, we had to have a grown-up conversation in front of you. Now we're gonna do it again. Even though you're only twelve, there might be some things you hear in the neighborhood, some ugly things that no child should even know about, but we can't help it. Seems like ugly has come and set up shop in Greenwood."

I stood there, unsure what I should do.

"Sit down, son."

As I eased into a chair, I snuck a glance at both Mama and Daddy. Daddy looked a little rough. Big bags under his eyes. The corners of his lips turned down. His eyes darted around, instead of his normal, steady gaze. His hands fidgeted with the salt and pepper shakers, and normally, when Daddy wasn't working on a car or fixing the sink or carrying my little sister around, his hands were still.

Some of Mama's hair was trying to run away from her scarf. She was wearing one of her oldest dresses. Her collar was frayed. And no makeup on. Oh, don't think my mama liked to get all dolled up just for us. She didn't. But usually she wore a little lipstick. Not today. Today her lips were the same color as her face. And her face looked a little paler than usual.

Daddy started talking. "I told you and Mama about Dick Rowland's trouble, about that White girl who said

49

he attacked her. He's in jail, but lots of White folks aren't happy about that. They think jail's too nice a place for him. They'd rather see him swingin' from a tree than livin' in a cell."

Thinking of somebody I knew, swinging from a rope, all lifeless...well, it made me shiver.

"I think you need to hear this 'cause you're a colored boy. Soon you'll be a colored man. And your mama and I try to impress on you that life for a colored man is rough. Colored men have to be extra careful in the way they talk to White folks, how they act around White folks, even how they look at White folks."

"Yes, sir."

"From what I hear, some of the preachers and business folk around here are gathering to try and keep this kid safe. There's probably nothin' to it. Probably all the talk about lynchin' is just that—all talk. But better safe than sorry. I figure I'll head over to the jail and see what's goin' on.

"And Margaret, I think Henry should go with me. You may not agree; you may fuss about it. But if there's a child around when this talk is takin' place, maybe everyone will remember their manners and be a little more civilized."

Me go with Daddy to this grown-up thing? Get to stand next to him like a man, and him thinking I'm an equal? I stopped breathing for a minute, as I looked at Mama.

She closed her eyes. This was another bit of strange on this strange day. Mama lived her life with her eyes wide open, always watching out for her family. I'd never seen something come along to make her shut her eyes and refuse to look at it.

When she opened them, she sighed. A big breath came out, like Mama'd been holding all her air in just like I had.

"What if something happens, James? You said it yourself. Those White folks might turn into a flood of rage. And just like you said, no one will be able to stop them.

"What'll happen to my boy then?" Mama put her hands on her hips and stared at Daddy, and it looked like she was about to cry. Her forehead wrinkled up, and her eyebrows pushed down on her eyelids.

"Margaret, it's just a talk. And I think it's just a talk amongst the colored preachers and some of the shop owners to see if we can head any trouble off before it gets a chance to get started." Daddy got up, went over, and hugged Mama, still standing there. She halfway hugged him back. Her face turned towards me without a smile.

Daddy kept a hold on her but pushed her away enough, so he could look at her. "I promise to keep him safe, sugar. Remember, he's my boy, too," and he grinned. I knew what Daddy was doing: sweet-talking Mama, trying to tease her into a smile.

It worked.

Mama teased him right back, although knowing Mama, it wasn't much of a joke. She was being more serious than funny. "James, you'd best keep that promise of yours 'cause if you don't and something happens to Henry, I'll haunt you til the end of your days. You hear me?"

Daddy leaned in and kissed her. "Loud and clear, mama bear."

Daddy was right. My mama was like a mother bear. Mess with one of her cubs, and the claws would come out. That was for certain.

Tuesday, May 31, 1921, 6:30 p.m.

I probably didn't look no different, but I sure felt different, as Daddy and I walked to the jail. I shoved my hands in my pockets, trying to match Daddy stride for stride, trying to let him know that I was gonna do my best to make him not regret this.

We didn't talk. Neither one of us said a word. I guessed that's what being a man was like. If there's no reason to say anything, you say nothing.

When we got about a block away, I heard a humming that echoed in my chest. Voices. Low. It sounded like a swarm of bees.

As we turned the corner, we saw a group of men milling in front of the courthouse. There were a dozen or so bunched up and talking. A couple of them were deputies or maybe the sheriff. They were wearing uniforms, and their badges glinted in the sunlight.

When we got right up on top of them, I saw the guns hanging from their belts.

One of the men, the preacher from our church, turned, saw my daddy, and said, "James. Good to see you." He and Daddy shook hands.

"Good evenin', Reverend Epps. What are you gentlemen talking about?"

"We're discussing young Mr. Rowland. It seems the boy's in a heap of trouble. So much trouble, they had to move him."

Daddy joined the circle. I stood behind him and off to the side. "Move him? Move him where?" Daddy asked and stared at Sheriff McCullough.

"As I was sayin'," the sheriff announced. "There are some folks who want to take the law in their own hands. A White girl attacked by a colored boy? Tempers are flaring. Folks in Tulsa aren't gonna be happy until that boy is lynched.

"I figured the jail cell, being here on the ground floor, is too close to the rabble-rousers, so my men moved the kid to the cell on the top floor of the courthouse. He's safe up there. I got a couple men guarding him. Burrell and Mason. Nobody's gonna get through them." The sheriff crossed his arms across his chest.

"Sheriff, we've been hearin' too many rumors. You know what they say—where there's smoke, there's fire. Things are heatin' up," said Mr. Palmer. I recognized him as owner of the barber shop.

Mr. Nash worked at the hardware store, but we hardly ever went there. He nodded and then boomed with his deep, loud voice, "I've been hearin' things, too. I'm kinda worried. When the White folks figure out Rowland's not here, what are they gonna do? Go on a wild rampage? Tear us up? Knock out your two deputies and then tear up Rowland? I'm sorry, Sheriff. I'm not as confident as you are."

Sheriff McCullough and his deputies were White, standing on the steps, surrounded by the colored men who had gathered. We'd never had any dealings with him, of course, but from what Mama and Daddy had said, he wasn't too bad of a guy. From what they read in the newspapers and what they heard from neighbors, it seemed like Sheriff McCullough tried to keep Greenwood peaceful and quiet.

The sheriff uncrossed his arms, reached into his pants pocket for his handkerchief, and noisily blew his nose. He sounded like a goose. I wanted to chuckle, but instead bit my lip before I started snickering. This was no time for laughter.

"Well, I'm confident in my men. They're trained. They know what to do. If any trouble comes this way, they'll be able to handle it."

The sheriff put his hands in his pockets and continued. "I think the best thing to do for now is for everybody to go home. Get on home, and don't worry about the prisoner. Let us do our job, and you folks just stay home and stay out of the way."

The circle of men didn't seem like they liked the sheriff telling them what to do. I looked at his gun again. It looked harmless there, hanging from his belt, but I'd heard enough from Mama and Daddy to know that nobody should argue with a gun.

I'd also heard enough to know that when it's a colored man against a gun and the gun's in a White man's hand, the colored man always loses.

Some of the men mumbled under their breath. Some of them shuffled their feet and cast their eyes downward. Daddy grabbed my shoulder and steered me away from the circle of men towards home.

We didn't talk on the way home either. I snuck a couple of quick peeks at Daddy and tried to figure what was going on in his mind. Was he still worried about a lynching that might happen? Was he worried if Dick Rowland was safe or not? Was Daddy mad that he and the other men had been treated like little boys being told to get home and stay inside?

No luck. His face was like a piece of granite.

Tuesday, May 31, 1921, 7:30 p.m.

Things were so mixed up, even dinner was late. Mama told us when we left that she'd wait dinner on us. She'd feed Livvie, but she would wait until the three of us could sit down together to eat.

When we got home, the smell of Mama's smothered chicken made my mouth water. Mama made some kind of sauce and covered the chicken up in that sauce and then baked it. She put lots of onions and red peppers and garlic in the sauce, and the whole house ended up smelling delicious.

While Mama set the table, Daddy filled her in on what had happened: the colored men were told to go home and stay out of the sheriff's way. The sheriff had moved Dick to what he thought was a safer place, and we couldn't do anything now except wait.

Dinner that night was a quiet one. Livvie didn't yammer on and on because she had already eaten and was playing in her room.

Daddy and Mama were quiet. Daddy was a big eater, which made him and Mama a great team 'cause Mama was a good cook. Most meals, Daddy ate fast and got seconds (and sometimes thirds).

Tonight, he ate a lot slower, and a couple of times, he pushed food around on his plate. If I did that, Mama would have scolded me to stop playing with my food.

I read for a while. Mama read some Bible stories to Livvie. Tonight it was the story of Noah and his ark, and they were making a big racket. The two of them were taking turns making all sorts of animal noises, as they pretended to be elephants and donkeys and ducks walking up the ramp to the ark. Mama, most times, read only one book to my sister, and then it was lights out. No questions and no arguing. Tonight was different.

Why did Mama keep reading? Every other night, after she finished reading to Livvie, Mama hurried to get to her mending or some other chore around the house. Why wasn't she in a hurry tonight? Why was she happy to lie down on Livvie's bed? After they finished with Noah and all his animals, they went on to another story. I couldn't hear what Mama was reading, just the two of their voices softly humming in unison.

What was going on with Dick Rowland? Did that worry Mama so much, she just wanted to get under Livvie's quilt and hide from the trouble? I listened to the drone of their voices as I read.

After a while I set my book down and looked at the alarm clock next to my bed. It was almost 8:30, still early, but Mama wanted me to do some work in the morning, so I needed to get up extra early—which meant I needed to get to sleep early.

When I headed to say good night to Daddy, I stopped and stepped out of the entryway and back into the shadows. Daddy was talking to somebody on the phone, and the way his voice sounded made me catch my breath and hold it.

"How many you say? A couple hundred outside the courthouse?" There was a break. I guessed he was listening to the caller's answer.

"What they want? Aw, who am I foolin'? I know what they want. We all know what they want. They want that boy hung and then cut up into little pieces."

I peeked around the corner of the doorway. Daddy nodded his head as he gripped the receiver against his ear.

"You headed to the courthouse?" Daddy paced back and forth in the kitchen. More silence. More listening.

"You are? Then I'll bring my Colt. Hope we don't have to use 'em."

Some more quiet. "Alright. I'll see you there."

Daddy put the receiver back on its cradle. I peeked again. Daddy was hunched over the kitchen table, doing something. Then he walked to the coat closet, got his pistol off the top shelf, and quietly left the house.

His gun? I hardly ever saw Daddy with his gun. Daddy went out in the woods sometimes with his brother when Uncle Franklin came into town. Uncle Franklin brought his rifle, and Daddy took his pistol; but usually, they wouldn't ever come back from the woods with anything. After those trips with his brother, Daddy came back home and told me, when Mama was out of earshot, "Sometimes, men just need some time away from the hens and all their peckin'. It ain't about the shooting or the huntin.' It's more about being with my brother."

59

I took a few steps towards Liv's room. I heard her and Mama back to making animal noises. As quietly as I could, I went into my room and put on some socks and shoes. I tiptoed down the hall and across the front room to the kitchen. As I snuck around, I tried to avoid the creaky spots on the floor.

What was Daddy doing when he was bent over in the kitchen? I found a piece of paper on the table with some scrawling on it. Daddy had left Mama a note. Another strange thing since as far as I knew, Daddy had never written a letter or a note. He was a man who did things. He tossed us up in the air when we were babies. He held Mama's hand in church. He kissed our knees when we skinned them up.

Taking the time to write a letter or note? That was not my daddy.

I leaned over the table to read it. It didn't even take half a minute because it was so short, although I could tell Daddy had tried to use his best handwriting.

Margaret,

I'm heading to the courthouse. Don't worry. I'll try not to be late.

Love you.

My worry about Daddy going out at night mixed with the picture in my head of him taking that pistol with him and all those White folks at the courthouse.

Under Daddy's note, I printed,

Mama, I went too. Don't be mad.

Henry

And I slipped out the front door, just minutes behind Daddy. I knew it was probably a bad thing to do, but I couldn't help it.

Tuesday, May 31, 1921, around 9:00 p.m.

Daddy had a big head start. As I walked down the dark street, he was nowhere to be seen.

The frogs were noisy. Their croaking kept me company as I kept an eye out for a grown-up who would see me and tell me to get on back home.

But nobody did. Nobody saw me.

As I headed towards the courthouse, off in the distance a train's whistle wailed on the railroad tracks that divided Tulsa into two sections: the White section and the Black section. It was strange, being able to step over train tracks and stepping into a different world, but that's how it was. On one side was Greenwood, where we lived. Where I got my hair cut. Where we got our groceries. Where we went to school and church, and where we were loved and respected.

On the other side was a world we entered only when we had to. A place where people called us nasty names. A place where we got ugly looks, where people moved to the other side of the street just to avoid us. A place where we were hated.

When I got to the corner by the courthouse, I heard voices. Angry voices. People arguing. A bunch of people talking at once.

When I rounded the corner and saw all those White folks yelling, the line of shoulder-to-shoulder deputies blocking the courthouse door, and a couple dozen colored men bunched together, I skidded to a stop. I couldn't find Daddy and scanning the faces didn't help. Finally, I recognized his plaid shirt. The small white rectangles let me know he was safe.

I took a few steps back and crouched behind a bush. Most of the White men were hollering at the sheriff and the deputies. The Black men stood off to the side, huddled together.

I couldn't make out what most of them were saying. I heard "that nigger" a bunch of times, and I trembled. It wasn't just the word. I'd heard that ugly word many times, but this time, there were lots of White men in the same spot, and I figured they were all thinking the same thing. With all those minds working together to spit out the same meanness, it was like a storm of hatred was brewing.

I heard somebody say, "Get back!" to a knot of men. A few of the White men said something, and then they stepped away from the courthouse door.

Their voices sounded like the angry saws at the sawmill—chewing up tree trunks, chopping up branches, destroying everything that got in their way.

More grinding. More yelling. More small groups swarmed together, broke apart, then reformed.

I kept an eye on Daddy. I sure didn't want him to know I was hiding behind a bush in the middle of the night, but if it looked like somebody was aiming to hurt him, I didn't care what kind of trouble I would get into later. I would run and kick and swing my fists for my daddy.

Sheriff McCullough said something, something I couldn't make out, something which made some of the colored men yell back. Then the sheriff shouted, "Boys, we don't need your help. Go on back home. Go on," and Daddy, along with the rest of the group he was huddled with, turned and headed my way.

Oh shoot. If Daddy got home, and I wasn't there, I would be in a heap more trouble. I knew I'd probably have a sore backside tomorrow for sneaking out of the house. But if I got home after Daddy got home, it would be worse.

The men were almost half a block away. I hightailed it home.

Tuesday, May 31, 1921, 10:15 p.m.

I could hear Mama pacing and fuming before I even opened the screen door. She snorted air in and out of her nose like a dragon about to burn down a village. I could tell right away she was madder than blue blazes.

When the screen door creaked open, I poked my head in. Mama stopped and whirled around, so her full glare hit me head-on.

"What in the world were you thinkin', Henry?" *Smack!* Mama hit me upside my head and then hugged me. She whispered in my ear, " I could have lost you. I could have lost you." Mama hit me on the head again—this time she didn't mean it—and said, "Where's your daddy? What happened out there?"

"I stayed around the corner, Mama, away from the courthouse. Nothing much happened. The colored men folks weren't allowed to do nothin' but stand around. The White men wanted to get at Dick Rowland. When the sheriff said—"

Daddy's deep voice, as he said good-bye to someone, interrupted me.

Mama let me go and rushed to the door. "James," she said, and Daddy hurried into the house.

"You had me worried sick. Leavin' with just a note, not telling me before you left. What happened at the courthouse?"

I looked at Mama and squinted my eyes, as I tried to puzzle out what was going on, but I knew better than to open my mouth and ask. She hadn't said a thing to Daddy about me sneaking out—yet. As a matter of fact, she was acting like she knew nothing about the goings-on at the courthouse. I would have expected her to start by telling Daddy about me sneaking out, to tear into me again in front of Daddy, so he could take his turn on me. But she didn't. She acted like we'd all been safe and sound, tucked in at home.

"Just a minute, Margaret. Let me go to the bathroom, and then I'll tell you all about it."

As soon as the bathroom door closed, Mama grabbed a hold of me again and whispered, "No need to worry your daddy any more than he already is. Your sneaking out—that's gonna be our little secret. Understand?"

I nodded. Mama was right. Daddy had been so worried tonight, his brow looked like it would never unwrinkle. I surely didn't want to add to his pile of worries.

Daddy sat down on the couch and looked at me, his eyebrows up and curious. "What's Henry doin' up? Why ain't he in bed?"

Thankfully, he didn't notice I had shoes on.

"Oh, he got up a few minutes ago, thirsty. He saw me up, didn't see you, and got to askin' questions." Mama put her arm around my shoulder. "I figured we might as well keep each other company while we waited up for you."

This was the first time I'd ever heard a lie come out of Mama's mouth. Neither of my parents had any tolerance for dishonesty. I guess there were times when it was okay to lie, and this was one of them.

"So what happened? Did the White folks get their way and get Dick Rowland?" Mama said, sitting next to Daddy.

I stood behind the rocking chair, figuring I'd get sent back to bed right away, so no point in sitting down and getting comfortable. But I was wrong. They let me stay.

"Naw, they didn't get hold of that kid. They tried to, but the sheriff put a line of his deputies between the White folks and the courthouse door. A bunch of us offered to help, but the sheriff didn't want no part of our help. There was some name-callin' directed our way from the White folks. Eventually, us colored men were sent home." Daddy rubbed his eyes in a rough way. "I don't think it was a good idea, Sheriff McCullough sending us home, but I suppose he's not interested in my opinion. If he did ask, I would have told him that I don't think the trouble's over yet." Daddy got up and stretched. "What say we all go to bed? It's late, and morning's right around the corner."

"Not so fast, James Henry Simmons."

Daddy sat back down, and I got still as a statue. When Mama called us by our first, middle, and last name, she was serious as a heart attack.

"You could have gotten hurt. Or killed!" Mama turned and stared at me. It seemed like she was sizing me up, like she was trying to figure if she'd gone too far. I looked right back at her, didn't look down, to let her know I'd grown up a lot over the last couple of hours. I wanted her to know I understood how dangerous it had been for Daddy to head out into a mob of White folks—which is why I snuck out after him. Maybe Mama had already figured that out, and that's why she was keeping it a secret from Daddy.

"Messin' with White folks when they're in the mood for blood? That was a hard-headed thing to do, James." She leaned over and kissed the side of Daddy's head. "Next time, you think about how many folks you got at home who love that hard head of yours before you run off and do something foolish again."

"Yes, ma'am," Daddy said and stood up again.

I went into the kitchen because now I really was thirsty, and as I walked by the table, I saw Daddy's note was gone. What had Mama done with it? He'd written it on a piece of grayish paper torn from Livvie's school tablet. When I finished with my glass, I put it in the sink. As I walked out of the kitchen, I glanced down.

There in the trashcan was a wadded-up piece of gray paper. I saw the distinctive red lines, lines that kept Livvie's loopy cursive letters where they should be.

That paper wad was proof that sometimes Mama strayed. That wadded-up piece of trash was proof that my mama didn't always walk the straight and honest path. I used to think things in life were either black or white, just like there were Black people and there were White people. The stuff I did was either right or wrong, or so I thought. But with Mama telling Daddy a lie—for a good reason—it made me realize that life was way more complicated than just good and bad. Maybe there were parts of life that were gray, parts that weren't completely right, but they're not exactly wrong either.

Tuesday, May 31, 1921, 11:00 p.m.

Reading at night before bed calmed me down. For the second time that night, I stretched out, doubled-up my pillow, and propped my book up on my wadded-up blanket. I figured Robinson Crusoe would follow me into dreamland.

Brrring. Brrring. It wasn't too long after I'd started reading. Phone calls late at night were never good. It was either serious sickness or a death, but with all that had been going on tonight, I almost knew for certain it was not a cousin who was sick or an auntie who'd died.

That phone was probably ringing about the goings-on at the courthouse.

I stepped into the hall and heard Daddy talking. It made me feel like I was in a moving picture show, and I was stuck in the same role doing the same thing over and over—eavesdropping on my daddy and trying to figure out what was happening to Dick.

"They're doing what? They're tryin' to break into the courthouse?"

Silence, while Daddy listened, I guessed.

"Yeah, it does sound like the sheriff needs our help. This time, he'd best not turn us away."

Daddy paused and then, "You're gonna pick me up?" Daddy was quiet for a moment. "I guess you're right—safety in numbers, safety in numbers. I'll be lookin' out the door for you, Joseph," he said and hung up the phone.

As quick as I could, I slipped back into my room, turned off my light, and shut my bedroom door most of the way. And then I stood there, still, as I tried to hear what Daddy was going to say to Mama.

It didn't work. Even with my door cracked and me breathing as shallow as I could, I still couldn't make out what Daddy said to Mama. He whispered to her; she whispered back. They did this back-and-forth hushed talk, and then I heard Daddy in the hall. I heard him cross our creaky front room floor and a moment later, I heard the rusty screen door open and shut.

Why didn't I run into the front room and ask him what was happening at the courthouse?

Probably 'cause I knew better. If Mama had caught me tiptoeing around again with more than half a mind to sneak out, for the second time in one night, I'd have ended up with a whole mess of bumps on my head.

A whole mess...

I tried to read for a while and must have then drifted to sleep. Because the next thing I knew, I was awakened by cracks so loud, they could only be one thing—gunshots.

Tuesday, May 31, 1921, 11:40 p.m.

There were so many gunshots for a while, it sounded like a war, probably like when Union and Confederate soldiers were lined up, facing each other, trying their best to destroy one another.

After I first heard the bullets fly, I scrambled out from the safety of my quilt and scooted underneath my bed. I lay there on my back, my face turned so if anybody walked in, I could spy on their feet.

The wooden floor felt cool against my arms. Because Mama was constantly sweeping and mopping, and because she probably checked under my bed every day to see if I had shoved something there in my haste to clean up, I was all alone, sandwiched under my bed springs. No baseball glove or shoes to shove aside. No clumps of dust to sneeze or sputter over. Just me.

I'd considered the corner. When I was Livvie's age, I always went to the corner when I was scared. Hunkered down, with two walls to hug me, somehow made me feel safer. Now that I was older, I knew a corner offered no protection at all.

There was no way a bullet could have been determined enough to go through my window, curve around and then go through my mattress and the curly-que wires in order to get to my flesh. At least I hoped not.

I shivered. When I'd rolled off my bed, I hadn't bothered to grab a sheet or my quilt. On the brink of summer, it usually wasn't this cool; but I was only in my pajamas, and a breeze was blowing through my open window. From where I was, I could see the edges of my curtains fluttering, making it seem like it was an ordinary night.

Many nights, I'd wake up and watch the flimsy curtains dance in the breeze. I'd study the moonlight streaming down on the floor, transforming my room into a mysterious place.

Never before had I heard gunshots in Greenwood like that. Oh, once in a while somebody got out of hand, folks whispered that he drank too much, and there'd be one or two pops. But usually we heard about that after the fact instead of hearing the actual pops. Greenwood was a peaceful place, so to have a war going on made sweat bead up on my arms, which made me even cooler once the breeze whispered over my skin.

Listening, I figured the shooting was far away, but I wasn't an expert. I'd gone hunting with Daddy a couple of times, and these explosive cracks sounded like the shots I might have heard if I was sitting in the car, and Daddy was several hills and fields away as he shot.

I also listened, waiting for Mama to wake up or for Livvie to wake up, crying. How long did I lie there, completely still? I wasn't sure. It seemed like hours.

"Mama! Mama!" Livvie screamed out.

I scooted out from under my bed and rushed out of my bedroom. As I passed by the nightstand, I glanced at my alarm clock. Thank goodness for the light of the moon streaming into my bedroom because I could see the time.

It was 12:08.

Wednesday, June 1, 1921, after midnight

I looked at my sister. "Ssssh, Livvie. Ssssh. It's okay." I almost told her, "Nothing's gonna hurt you," but I wasn't sure that was true. I just knew that, at that moment, we were both okay.

My baby sister was so wide awake and scared, when I'd hurried into her room, she was sitting straight up. Her eyes looked startled, like a wild horse. Even in her dark room, I could see lots of the white part of her eyes, and her pearly teeth, as she cried out. I grabbed a hold of her.

"Mamaaaa!"

"Hey, sis. It's okay. I'm here," I said, but it wasn't me she wanted. Right that minute, I don't think Daddy would have even made her happy. Only Mama could quiet her down.

I hugged her tighter. She did her best to push me away and was still making a racket.

"Maybe we should go see Mama? Would you like that, Livvie?" I leaned back enough to see her nod. Her crying got a little quieter.

Grabbing her hand, along with her baby doll Minnie, I helped her out of bed, and we shuffled down

77

the hall. There was a crack of light coming from the bottom of Mama and Daddy's door. That was strange. Neither one of them liked to stay up late. I wondered if Daddy had just gotten back from his third trip out tonight.

Maybe they were up just like Livvie and me. Maybe they were up trying to figure out where all the shooting was happening. Knocking softly on the door, I whispered, "Mama? Daddy? Is it okay to come in?"

Mama opened the door and said, "Is she sick?" as she reached down and grabbed up my sister.

"No, I don't think so. Livvie and I both got woken up by...well, you know." I sure didn't want to say "gunshots" or "bullets" and make Livvie even more upset. But when I looked at Mama, her face was blank. Almost like she hadn't heard me. Almost like she hadn't even heard the gunshots. How could that be?

"Mama, I think Livvie just wants to get in bed with you and Daddy. She woke up scared, is all."

"Oh. Okay," but there was no feeling in Mama's voice as she stood there with my sister in her arms, and she didn't move towards the bed.

Then my brow furrowed up, and I tilted my head to one side, so I could see around Mama. What was going on?

Mama and Daddy's bed was still made up. The quilt was smoothed down, not a wrinkle anywhere. I glanced around their bedroom. No sign of Daddy, but I did notice an afghan wadded up on Mama's rocking chair.

When coming in here, I hadn't noticed any light on in the family room or the kitchen, and the bathroom was empty. So before this moment, I'd figured Daddy must have been in their bedroom with Mama. But there was no sign of him. My gut sank. Was Daddy at the courthouse still with all those gunshots?

I stared at her, trying to put the puzzle pieces together. A bed that hadn't been slept in. A chair that looked like it had been slept in. And Mama's face was as blank as a new piece of paper.

"Is Daddy still at the courthouse?" My question came out before I could stop it. I wasn't supposed to know about the late-night phone call—the last time Daddy went to the courthouse. I wasn't supposed to know that Daddy left to help Dick Rowland again.

Mama looked away and mumbled something. She didn't even react to me saying something about Daddy going to the courthouse. Maybe I wasn't gonna get in trouble for this one.

"Excuse me, Mama? What did you say?"

She turned back towards me, and we locked eyes. She stared at me, her face like part of a tree. There were deep grooves worn around her mouth and on her forehead, like the bark on the trunk, but nothing on her face moved.

"I said, 'I guess he's at the courthouse,' but I don't know. I just don't know."

I looked at Mama, my eyes narrowed. My chest got tight all of a sudden.

"Mama, what don't you know?"

"You asked if your daddy was still helping out at the courthouse. I'm sure he is." And then she looked away, trying to hide the fact that her lower lip had started to quiver.

"I just don't know how we're gonna manage until he gets back—and I don't know when he's gonna come home."

Wednesday, June 1, 1921, 12:30 a.m.

Mama's tone did not make me feel any better. "What do you mean, you don't know when Daddy's coming home? He left a little bit ago. He should be back real soon, because—" I stopped talking. I wasn't supposed to have known of Daddy's third trip, and although I got away with mentioning it a few minutes ago, I needed to calm down.

But I quickly saw I didn't have to worry about Mama getting angry over me being nosy. It was as if she were surrounded by a cocoon of thick, cottony clouds. She didn't frown or look worried. When a tear leaked out, it seemed like she didn't even know it was happening. What I said to her—I wasn't completely sure she heard me or if she understood what I said. What she said to me—it seemed like talking took more energy than she had, like it was all she could do to mumble. Moving her mouth any more would have been too much for her.

She still held Livvie, but Mama hung onto her like my sister was a sack of potatoes. Lucky for Liv, all my little sister needed was to be close to Mama because as soon as she had gotten picked up, she stopped crying and fell back to sleep.

The shooting continued. The popping kept on. Mama stared off to the side of me, like she was watching something many miles away.

Then it hit me. I knew why Mama had been in her rocking chair instead of in bed. She and Daddy had never spent a night apart. On a regular night, Mama and Daddy went to bed together. From my room, I could hear them. Clicking off the lights. Closing the front door. Whispering to each other as they made their way down the hall and into their room. Their door quietly getting shut. Mama wasn't going to go to bed until Daddy was beside her.

She wasn't acting like Mama because she and Daddy were glued to each other, and without him, part of her was missing. The way she stared right through me, like I wasn't even there? I knew why. Mama couldn't see a life without Daddy. Just the very thought probably terrified her, but I understood what she was feeling because it frightened me, too.

What if Daddy didn't come back today? What if he spent the next couple of days helping Dick Rowland stay safe, and all the while, we didn't know what's happening to him? Was Mama going to be able to stand up and be Mama and Daddy until he returned to us?

I tried to force her into seeing me and hearing me. I tried to make her get back to being Mama. "Didn't the phone ring after I went to bed? At least I thought I heard it." The state Mama was in, I figured she wouldn't remember that I'd already admitted I knew the answer to this question.

"Oh, yes. Joseph Chappelle called." Mama sat down on her rocking chair. "He told your daddy there was trouble still at the courthouse. A mob of White men were stirring things up at the courthouse." Then she muttered something else, something I couldn't quite hear. All I could catch was the word "slip."

"Mama, I couldn't hear that last part. What did you say about slipping?"

Instead of answering right away, she wrapped the afghan around Livvie and herself and rocked. A couple more gunshots. Mama didn't even flinch. I watched her while she stared out the window, even though there was nothing to see since the curtains were drawn shut. "What was that last thing you said, Mama?"

"Those White folks won't be happy until they can slip a noose around that Rowland boy's neck," and she kept rocking and looking at nothing, at least nothing I could see. Then she added, "Your daddy can fix lots of things, but this is something I don't think even he can fix."

I stood there for a while, then I sat on the edge of Mama and Daddy's bed. I figured soon she'd fuss at me to get up. Neither one of them cottoned to Livvie or me being in their bed. Not when I was little. Not when we were sick. Children belonged in their own beds, not crowding out the grown-ups, according to them, but the fussing never happened tonight.

And I was beat—from the phone calls and going to the jail and then later following Daddy, and then all the shooting, and Livvie waking up screaming, I was barely able to keep my eyes open. My lids kept drooping down, and each time I had to flutter them open.

If I lay down for a while, I could watch over Mama and maybe find out why she was acting like she was.

Unfortunately, the thinking side of my brain lost out to the sleepy side because not even a minute after my head met Mama's pillow, I was asleep. I think I'd blinked a couple of times, trying to focus on Mama and Livvie while they rocked, and then I didn't remember another thing.

Until the siren.

Wednesday, June 1, 1921, 5:08 a.m.

A high-pitched whistle or siren woke me up. Had the bullets been flying all night? I wasn't sure. When I sat up with a start, it looked like Mama had dozed off, and the siren had jolted her awake, too. She held onto Livvie with one hand and wiped the sleep out of her eyes with the other one.

"What in the world was that?" Mama said. One eyebrow was up. Mama was staring at me, not through me. Finally. Finally Mama was acting like Mama. Obviously, she'd heard the same thing I did, and she was just as puzzled about it as I was.

"I don't know, Mama. Never heard it before." No church I'd ever heard had a bell that sounded like that, and it wasn't a cornet or a trumpet, either. A kid's toy whistle wasn't that loud because whatever it was, it seemed like that sound was blocks and blocks away... and still it drifted into our house, powerful enough that it jolted us awake with a single, long blast.

The gunshots were popping off faster than they were when I'd first come into Mama's room. It still sounded like what I thought the North and the South shooting at each other might have sounded like, back in 1860-something.

It wasn't just single shots anymore. There were some far-off *bratatatatatatats*, too. I didn't say anything to Mama, but I would have bet anything that some bigger, more powerful gun made that noise.

But when I saw Mama's eyes, as round as pie plates, I knew that she knew what that sound was, too.

"Why don't we act like we're camping out? We'll spread some blankets on the floor and put all our pillows down to make it nice and comfy," Mama said. Livvie was half-awake now, so I hurried into my room and got my blanket and top sheet, along with my pillow and Livvie's quilt and her pillow, and spread them out on Mama and Daddy's braided rug.

Mama gestured for me to lie down first, then she carefully put Livvie down next to me. She nestled Minnie the doll in Livvie's arms. Once my sister snuggled up to the first warm body she found—me—and held onto her doll with one hand and me with the other, Mama curled up to serve as a wall between anything that might fly through her window and us. She folded her hands and quietly prayed.

I closed my eyes and let out a big breath as I wound Livvie's arms around me to keep her close. I was still tired, but I was more tired of trying to act like a man. Machine guns in Greenwood? Were we gonna get shot in our own home? That was stuff a 12-year-old boy shouldn't have had to worry about.

I was glad Mama was back to being Mama, so I could go back to being a kid.

My eyes closed, and I fell asleep again. I was so tired; the gunshots couldn't keep me from sleeping. And me? I couldn't keep the bad dreams away.

A circle of White faces surrounded me. In front of each face was a pistol aimed at me. I shivered and shook. I begged them to let me go, but they didn't say a thing. They just stood there, glaring at me.

The circle of men was so tight, I looked, but there was no gap for me to squeeze through and make an escape.

All together, they cocked their pistols. I started blubbering like a baby, knowing this was going to be my last moment on earth. After making a warm river down my legs, a yellow puddle formed at my feet. Jesus. Mama. Daddy. God. I'm scared. I'm too young to die.

But then Daddy broke the links in the circle, his brown face shoving past the white ones. His meaty hands grabbed onto me, and instantly, I felt safe. Somehow, he folded my body into his, as he made himself into a shield. We pushed out of that ring of White people with me in my daddy's arms.

My dream shifted to the park. It was just me and Daddy, playing catch. His arms, ropy with muscles. Throwing the ball right to me, sometimes with such power, my palm burned like I had set it on the hot stove.

"What do you want to be when you grow up, son?"

Thwok. The baseball popped into my glove. "You know, Daddy, I'd love to be like Dobie Moore or Rube Currie. Having hundreds of people chanting my name, 'Henry! Henry!' while they stomp and clap." I stared at the ball, admiring the curved line of stitching around the leather. "Well, maybe I'd rather be like Dobie Moore, and be a great shortstop 'cause it seems like the whole game falls onto the pitcher's shoulders. I mean,

I want people to applaud when I step onto the field. I want cheers. I don't want no jeers."

Daddy threw the ball to me again. Because of the way we were faced up against each other (me in a little dip, Daddy on a slight hill) and because in my dream, it was close to sunset and the sun was getting ready to disappear out of sight, Daddy blocked out the sun for a moment.

"Boy, you know baseball's a team sport, right? The game is lost by all the men, or it's won by all the men. When one player stands alone, he can't play every position by himself. He has to depend on the other ball players." I watched as Daddy stood still for a moment as he rotated the ball in his hand, fingering the seams and the smoothness of the worn leather.

"But I know what you mean. Everybody's watching the pitcher so many times during the game. It ain't no fun when everybody's eyes are on you, and you mess up."

Thwok. That one was a real hand-burner. "Do you think I got a chance, Daddy? You think I might someday be a famous baseball player?"

"Henry, I don't know. I can't see that far down the road. What I do know is dreamin' big can't hurt. Your mama and I want you and Liv to dream as big as the sky. We want you to reach toward the stars." *Thwok*. That time, it was my turn to have thrown it perfectly. The sound of leather meeting leather echoed through the deserted park.

"Or maybe I want to grow up and be a famous writer like Paul Laurence Dunbar. Miss Marion had each one of us pick one of his poems and recite it. Some of them sounded more like songs than poems."

Daddy tossed the ball back to me, and I fingered the bump of the seams.

"Son, whether you make a living throwing a baseball or holding a pen, you got to remember dreaming big takes a lot of hard work. Sometimes it takes years and years to make that dream come true—and sometimes, that dream never comes true."

My eyes scrunched up, and furrows filled my brow. He knew me so well. I didn't have to say a word.

"I once saw a big ol' fancy house when I was about your age. It belonged to some rich White family. That moment, I decided that when I was all grown up, I'd live in a house like that." Daddy smiled.

"Well, you know how that dream ended, don't you? I got a small house instead of some drafty mansion, and I had to work like a dog just to get that. Still got to work hard and long every day. But that dream hasn't died. Not yet. It's just changed. Once in a while, I think of someday seeing you livin' in a big, fancy house. I see Olivia enjoying herself, as she's cutting roses in some beautiful flower garden, instead of having to rush around cooking and scrubbing, like Mama has to. That's the dream that keeps me going these days."

Did I travel somewhere during my sleep? I didn't know. All I knew was that when I woke up, I looked around, hoping to see that Daddy had come home, and we had just had that conversation. It felt so real. But no, we were on the floor with gunshots zinging around outside…and still no Daddy in sight.

Wednesday, June 1, 1921, 6:30 a.m.

The shooting was now constant enough to wake us and keep me and Mama both awake. And guns weren't making all the commotion. Something else had added to the noise.

Nnneeooowww. Nnneeooowww. There was only one thing that made that noise—planes—and they were close. Sometimes, it even sounded like they were right overhead, like they were low enough to scatter the dust on our roof.

And it sounded like there was more than one plane. There were several engines whining above us. Were they crisscrossing over our neighborhood? And if they were, why?

In Greenwood, we hardly ever heard or saw an airplane. One time in the country, we saw a plane flying over a farmer's field. I could see the propellers twirling around, a gray blur, and it made me think of how fast the wind must move way up in the sky. The pilot did some fancy tricks, like dip the wings, first the right and then the left, as if he was saying hello to everybody stuck on the ground.

Somehow, I knew these planes in Greenwood today were up to no good. Too many strange sounds for any of them to make sense. Gunshots plus machine guns spraying bullets plus low-flying airplanes?

Miss Marion had started teaching us algebra. We were learning how to solve equations with an unknown variable. You know, problems like $x + 9 = 21$, and we had to figure out what x was equal to.

We were practicing figuring out what those unknown numbers were. But lying on the floor with Livvie and Mama curled up with me, there were so many scary things that I couldn't figure out.

Too many things were unknown. And maybe, if somebody had given me a choice, I would have chosen to never find the answers to all I didn't know on that early Wednesday morning.

But nobody gave me that choice.

Because Mama and I were both done sleeping, our shifting around halfway woke up Livvie.

Mama had gotten up and walked, hunched over, into the hallway. There was a good-sized window in the kitchen, so I imagined her staying crouched down, as she figured out what we were going to have for breakfast.

Just because there were strange things going on, what with the gunshots and the airplanes that must have been flying low over our heads, didn't mean we should bypass breakfast. In fact, since trouble seemed to be bubbling over, eating breakfast was even more necessary.

When would the shooting stop? When would Daddy get home? When would Greenwood go back to being calm and peaceful?

"Where's Mama?" Livvie asked as she tried to roll away from me. She couldn't. Liv was wedged between me and Mama and Daddy's bed.

Trying to scoot down the length of me, since she couldn't get over me, didn't work either. "Livvie, come here." How was I going to distract my baby sister? Then I remembered the story Mama made up when we settled onto the floor.

"Livvie, we've been pretending like we're camping. Sleeping under the stars, stretched out on blankets on the hard ground. You might not have even realized it. You've been snoozing away. Well right this very minute, Mama is at the campfire, cooking us breakfast over an open fire. Let's just relax, and try to figure out what she's cooking up, just from the smells." I rubbed Livvie's back and scanned her face, trying to figure out if my plan had worked.

Her eyes and her mouth smiled. She pursed her lips and tilted her head to one side, which she always did when she was trying to think. Lucky Liv. Hours ago, she'd been woken up by gunshots, but she was too young to have realized what they were. She'd missed out on the airplanes. She was lucky, and she believed my lies.

"I think it's gonna be oatmeal. Now your turn. What's your guess?"

Livvie said, "That's not fair. I don't smell oatmeal. Does oatmeal even have a smell?"

I chuckled. Leave it to my sister to make this into a contest, which led her to claim I was cheating. "Now that you say that, Livvie, I realize you're right. Oatmeal doesn't really put off an aroma. However, I heard the faucet. Mama might have been filling the pot with water. I heard the stove, so I know it's not toast. And

93

you want to know what my third clue was?" I figured the more I could string her along, the longer she'd be happy to stay here where it was safe.

"Tell me. Tell me!"

I rubbed her back, something that Mama had done hundreds of times at bedtime to calm me down or to comfort me. "Well, I heard something metal scrape against a shelf in the cupboard. You know how Mama's been fussing about wanting to line the shelves with pretty paper, instead of having just bare wood? That bare wood makes a peculiar sound when something gets pulled off a shelf."

Pursing my lips and looking up at the ceiling, just to tease my sister, I made my eyes wide open, like I was thinking of something complicated. "So, either we're having canned spinach for breakfast, or Mama just got the oatmeal canister from the cupboard."

Livvie grinned, which for a moment made me forget the worries that were piling up in my head.

I went with my sister into the hall, so she could pee and wash her hands, and by the time we were finished, Mama was bringing in glasses of milk and spoons.

"We're eating in your room, Mama? Really?" Livvie's squeal was so high, it almost made me wince. Almost.

"I told Liv you were cooking our breakfast over a campfire. You know, after we slept under the stars," and then I winked so only Mama could see, and she fell right in line with my lies.

"Of course, we're eating here, right next to our bedrolls. Why don't the two of you set out the spoons and the milk while I keep an eye on the oatmeal?" Mama walked out again, stooped over. My sister's mouth gaped open in amazement.

"Henry, you were right!"

I couldn't stop myself. "Livvie, I'm always right." I hoped I wasn't right about the middle-of-the-night goings on. I hoped I was wrong about so many people shooting that it was like it was some war. I hoped I was wrong about that being machine guns I heard. And I hoped that the feeling in my stomach, that the planes flying right over our heads were there for a bad reason? I hoped that feeling was completely wrong.

In a little while, Mama brought in three bowls of oatmeal. In the middle of each mound of the sticky cereal was a big chunk of butter on its way to melting. Along with the butter was a splash of milk, along with some brown sugar and cinnamon.

Livvie started to grab her bowl and get up, so she could sit on Mama and Daddy's bed and eat, but Mama put an end to that in no time. "Olivia Sophia Simmons. Just who do you think you are, the Queen of Sheba? Daddy and I don't even eat in our bed." On another day, Mama would have been truly furious. Genuinely breathing fire. This time, it was just an act. There was a little false heat in her words, but no bite.

"Besides, Henry and I are eating around the campfire. Aren't you going to join us, baby girl?" Mama sat Minnie up, to eat along with us, to entice Livvie. I saw Mama run her eyes between the window and her bed a couple of times as my sister plopped down on the floor. If Liv was sitting up on the bed, she would have been right in line with the window.

Bullets. Windows. The shooting didn't sound like it was on our block, but when I'd go hunting with Daddy, he told me bullets can travel a long way. Out in the woods, trying to shoot a deer or a rabbit for food? That bullet traveling a long distance was a good thing, right?

As it went across a field and hit its target, that meant the hunter could bring home food to feed his family.

Who was hunting who in Greenwood right now?

Wednesday, June 1, 1921, 7:05 a.m.

We ate the oatmeal without much conversation. What were we supposed to talk about? The fact that we slept and ate on the floor? About all the commotion going on outside? About the fact that Daddy was gone?

That last topic was carefully and completely skirted around until Livvie brought it up.

First Liv asked about the gunshots, but Mama lied. "I think they might be firecrackers, sweetie."

My sister seemed to not even think twice about it even though we'd never heard firecrackers except on the Fourth of July.

Then she said, "Where's Daddy at?"

Mama caught my eye and shook her head so gently, I was the only one who noticed it. "Liv, he went to work early. But if Daddy was here, what would he say about the oatmeal still in our bowls?"

"Eat it, don't waste it," my little sister and I said it together. We'd heard it often enough. Daddy had no patience with either one of us failing to eat until our plates were clean. In his mind, it was hard-earned money going down the drain, and it was a waste of Mama's time since she worked hard to cook our meals.

As we were spooning up the last of our breakfast, something in my chest started pounding. It was a sound, but I felt it more than heard it.

"What in heaven's name is that?" Mama whispered so low and quiet I almost couldn't hear her.

At first, it felt like one or two horses galloping on a dirt road. In less than a minute, it was like a whole herd had joined the first two horses. The floor shook. The very air seemed to vibrate with an energy.

It was like the ground was jumping up and down, over and over.

"I'm gonna see what is going on outside. You two, stay here. Don't move," Mama said, and then she hunch-backed her way out of her bedroom and down the hall.

The pounding got louder. It felt like the herd of horses had gotten even larger. Sometimes train cars full of cattle passed through Tulsa. Could there be a train wreck, and the train cars full of cattle had gotten loose?

Was it people? Where were they running to? Or were they running away from something? My mouth went dry.

Livvie jolted me out of my wondering. "I wanna see what Mama's doing," she said.

I held Minnie up in the air, letting her dangle from my hand. The doll's arms waved, as I gently shook the doll. "And leave baby Minnie behind? Why don't you stay here and tell me all about what you and Minnie did yesterday?" I figured that would get her. My little sister loved talking about herself. I mean, she really loved getting the chance to be the star and be in the spotlight whenever she could. Most of the time, I did my best to ignore the little pest, but right now, I needed to be more than a big brother. I needed to step up and take Daddy's place until he came home.

While Livvie yammered, my mind wandered. First, I stared at the doll. Minnie's face was a mixture of colors—cream, light brown, and darker browns—and it was a splotchy mess. Even her eyes weren't quite right. They were black, but tiny specks of blue showed through.

I remembered a couple of Christmases ago, when Livvie asked for a baby doll. Daddy had gone shopping in Tulsa to find the perfect doll, but all he found were white dolls with blue eyes.

When he brought it home, he and Mama talked about it after Livvie had gone to bed. I was doing my homework at the same table the doll was on, and I was being as nosy as I could while I worked on my math problems.

"Margaret, this is the nicest doll I could find, at least the nicest doll that's meant to be played with. They don't have no brown baby dolls. Liv's just going to have to learn to love a white doll."

"Oh, James." Mama picked up the doll and stared into its plastic eyes. She ran her fingers through the long, brown hair. "It seems like there's something we could do to make this doll nicer for Livvie."

"What about shoe polish? Could you paint her face brown with shoe polish?" I said. I didn't say it too loudly because I didn't want it to be obvious I'd horned in on their conversation. I hunched even more over my math book to make myself as invisible as possible.

"Hey, that's a good idea, son." Daddy slapped me on my back and went to get our shoeshine kit. Soon Minnie was browner than she was white. Mama went to work like a painter as she dabbed brown shoe polish onto the doll's face, hands, and feet. (The rest of the doll was cloth, filled up like a pillow.) She took black polish and covered those blue eyes, using an old toothbrush.

And her long brown hair? Mama cut that off until it was short all over. She couldn't make it stand out or make it kinky-curly, but she did her best.

The three of us thought the doll was one big mess, but Livvie fell in love with that doll the minute she unwrapped her on Christmas morning. She immediately named her Minnie, and they'd been inseparable ever since.

Mama interrupted Livvie's yammering and my time-traveling to the past. "Henry. Livvie. Come here." When we got to the front room, Mama clutched her robe to keep it closed, and she opened the front door as a blur passed by our house.

"What is it, Mama? What's going on?" I held onto Livvie's hand.

"I don't know. People are running; they're all running. It looks like all of Greenwood is racing somewhere. They look like they're scared of something." Mama put her arm around me, and she guided us out the door. Once we got outside, she said, "You two stay on the stoop. Don't move an inch. You hear me?"

We both nodded. This time, there was nothing fake about the fierceness in her voice. Mama meant it.

People were running through the yards. Ladies in their nightgowns. Men in their pajama bottoms and nothing else. Children slung over their mamas' and daddies' shoulders like sacks of potatoes. Crying.

Yelling. Folks with their eyes wide open with so much white showin', they were looking like spooked horses.

All Livvie and I could do, standing side by side, was stare, as we wondered what was making everybody run scared.

I saw Eunice, a girl from school, running across our yard.

"Eunice! What's goin' on?" I shouted at her.

And then I smelled it before she even said it.

"They're burnin' Greenwood down," she shouted over her shoulder, and she kept on running.

I looked at Mama as she turned to look at me. Her eyes were wide open, making her look just like the people who were running through the yards and jumping over bushes and trampling flower beds.

The whole street had gone crazy.

As I puzzled the pieces together, Mama pulled us with her into the yard. Her arm was around my shoulder. My hand was on her hip, and we moved together like links on a chain—across the yard, past the bushes, and into the street. People flowed around us, like a flood of water around a big rock. We were smack dab in the middle of it, and we still didn't know what it was.

Eunice was right. Our noses told us faster than our eyes did. Our noses knew what it was. The smell of lots and lots of wood burning curled up into my nostrils.

And from somewhere in Greenwood, the air was smoky.

Wednesday, June 1, 1921, 7:30 a.m.

Mama pushed us through the front door after we rushed through our yard, then shut it— hard. "Get back inside."

Her eyes darted around. "We're gonna have to get some stuff together in case we have to leave." She grabbed onto my forearm with enough of a squeeze, it hurt. "If the White folks are burning down the shops in Greenwood, the houses might catch. We gotta be ready."

Her head swiveled around, making her look like one of those whirligigs some folks had in their yards. "Henry, get yourself and Olivia dressed, then go get her wagon from the backyard, and bring it inside. And Olivia? After you get dressed, gather all the blankets and quilts from our rooms. Pile them onto the sofa, and then sit on the floor in the kitchen." Mama rushed off towards the hall.

Bump! Bump! Bump! I dragged the red wagon across the grass and through the back door. As it rolled into the kitchen, the wagon's wheels trailed in dirt.

I didn't think I'd get fussed at for messing up Mama's floor, what with airplanes and guns and fires surrounding us. I smiled a halfway smile. Never ever did I ever get away with tromping in mud or bits of grass onto Mama's clean floor. Today was a first.

Of course, it was a first in lots of ways. I'd never felt unsafe in Greenwood. The corner of Archer and Greenwood was the heart, and all the other streets— Latimer, Marshall, King, Frankfort along with the rest of the streets in Greenwood—were like arms embracing me. I might not have known everybody that lived on the blocks around us, but we all greeted each other. And if I fell in front of a stranger's house, if I got into some kind of trouble, I knew somebody would come out and clean me off and bandage me up or help me get out of the scrape—as long as that stranger lived in Greenwood.

It was the first time I had seen Mama crumble in my life. Livvie and I had two rocks to depend on: Mama and Daddy. Our mama was always strong and always fearless. If we had a question or a problem, she had the answer, the solution. To see her looking scared, so scared she was frozen in place—that petrified me.

It was the first time I hated being treated like a grown-up. When Daddy took me hunting, when he and I went to the Monarchs ball game, when he took me along with him to the jail, my chest puffed out so much, I worried I'd bust out of my shirt. For as long as I could remember, I was chomping at the bit to be treated like a man. What I'd found out was being a man was not something I should try to hurry up. Just doing it for a little while these past twelve hours tired me out and worried me something awful. It wasn't fun at all.

It was also the first time Daddy had ever spent the night away from us, and we didn't know where he was.

It wasn't long before Mama had gotten dressed and came back into the front room with a bag. There were bulgy corners of things poking into the cloth of the sack. I didn't know what was in the bag. I didn't ask.

She grabbed the blankets and quilts and folded them up. She fit them neatly into the bed of the wagon, and she then got Daddy's work thermos out of the cupboard and filled it up with water. The thermos, along with a sack of leftover biscuits, went into the wagon too, right next to the mystery bag.

"Henry, take the wagon back out, put it close to the flower bed, then come right back in."

When I finished, Mama and Livvie were sitting next to the window in the front room. "Come sit with us," Mama said.

I sat cross-legged on the floor.

Right outside, on the other side of the wall I leaned against, the running continued. The ground continued to shake. People screamed. The gun shots slowed but hadn't stopped.

Mama let out a slow, long breath. "I know we've had a strange morning. It's morning still, I know, but I feel like I'm ready to go back to sleep." She leaned over and gave us each a kiss.

"We might have to leave for a little while—just to be safe. That's what the wagon's for. There are things in it that will tide us over for the next couple of hours until we can come home. In the meantime, we're just gonna keep an eye on things."

Livvie wiggled around, trying to get settled. "If we leave, how will Daddy know where we are?" she said.

Smoothing my sister's hair down, Mama said, "We're not leavin' for good, Liv. We'll just be gone for a little while. We'll leave, and when we get back, we'll get to hear what all your daddy has been up to."

Would Daddy be back when we got back? He'd been gone a long time. Had he gotten hurt? Were the men all standing guard, all night, to protect Dick Rowland?

Mama was right about one thing: Daddy would have a good story to tell us. Even after a regular day at work, Daddy could take what happened and put a funny twist on things.

"We're just gonna sit here, snug as a bug in a rug, and keep an eye on things. How does that sound, Olivia?" As Mama asked my little sister, she looked over Livvie's head at me. She had her hands up by her throat, holding onto something. Something glinted at me. There was a flash of gold, and then I saw what she was clutching.

Her locket. Daddy had gotten it for Mama a few years ago. She hardly ever wore it, only on special occasions. When she did hang it around her neck, she had on one of her Sunday best dresses. The last time I noticed her wearing her locket, she had on a pink dress with lace, high heels, and a hat with a net-like thing hanging over part of her face.

Did I miss something? Was she all gussied up now, and I'd missed it? No. This morning, she had on one of her everyday dresses. The hem was a little worn. The flowers on the fabric were a lot faded. I could tell she had scrubbed the collar many times to get it as white as it still was.

Where was Mama planning on us going, that she thought she needed to wear something fancy like her gold locket?

For a while we sat there. A few minutes? An hour? Still, we could hear people running through the streets. There was some yelling, but too far away for us to hear what they were saying.

Mama crooked a finger and pulled a bit of the curtain back, so she could peek out. I kept an eye on her face, trying to tell what she was seeing just by the expression on her face.

When her eyes got round as pie pans, I scooted over til I could see, too, and rested my head on Mama's shoulder. Livvie had gotten busy play-feeding Minnie. She had no idea that anything scary was going on. She'd believed that "snug as a bug" stuff.

My jaws clenched up. What I saw made my armpits swampy all of a sudden.

"Ssssh. Hush," Mama whispered, even though I hadn't said anything.

Halfway down the block, moving in a swarm like a dark cloud, was a bunch of White men. There were some women there, too, standing close to a truck. White women. There was another couple of trucks parked close by as well.

We watched as some of the men broke away from the group and headed into a house. The Roosevelts' house. The men tromped up onto the porch and didn't even bother knocking. It looked like they fiddled with the doorknob, and then we heard some glass break.

One of the men climbed through the window and then let the other ones in. They even left the front door hanging wide open.

What were they doing? And were the Roosevelts still there?

Two of the men came out, bent under a couch, as they carried it out into the street.

"These darkies have better things than I got," one of the men said. "That ain't fair!"

One of the men who had stayed in the street, talking, walked around the couch, ran his hand over it, and said, "What else they got?"

"Come on and see," one of the men who'd been in the house said to the whole group. "You can get yourselves somethin'."

"We can get ourselves a souvenir—somethin' to remember this morning," one of them said. A couple of the men hooted.

"Yeah, 'cause if we don't take it, it's just gonna burn!" a big-bellied man said and then laughed. A few others joined in.

"You got that right!" one of the White men said. He started staggering towards the house. The rest of them followed.

"Mama," I whispered. "This is wrong. Stealing? Breaking in and helping themselves to the Roosevelts' things? Shouldn't we do something? Shouldn't we call the sheriff?"

Mama shook her head, put her finger up to her lips, and again said, "Sssh."

Like ants heading to a pile of breadcrumbs on the sidewalk, the men trailed after each other, in and out, trip after trip. They hauled out the Roosevelts' dining room table and chairs. They dragged out their rocking chair. They started to bring out the Roosevelts' china. One man said they'd toss the plates up in the air and shoot them, but the women yelled at them and put an end to the men's plans.

"This ain't no shooting range," said one of the women.

Another woman said, "Do you think us ladies want to run around, dodging sharp bits of plates? No thank you."

Some of the men were drinking, I guessed, because I saw a bottle passed around. There was lots of staggering and lots of snorting and shoving each other—all in fun.

Their idea of fun.

I kept my voice low. We could hear these loud folks halfway down the block because it was spring, and our windows were open, but I sure didn't want them to hear us. "If we call the sheriff, they can put a stop to this, Mama. I mean, that's what they do. They stop criminals, and those folks surely are—"

She stopped me by grabbing onto my arm, and hissed at me. Low, quiet, but full of venom. "Boy, you think the sheriff is gonna stop those White folks? Those White folks are gonna get to do whatever they please. There's nothin' we can do. Nothin'." She leaned over and kissed me on the forehead, which let me know Mama's bitterness wasn't being blasted my way—it was directed at the people stealing stuff from the Roosevelts' home.

The big pieces of furniture got loaded into the trucks. It seemed like once the men were finished, it was time for them to take a break, smoking and drinking and joking around. Then, the White women had their turn.

Those White ladies looked like nice, law-abiding ladies. If I had seen them walking along on the sidewalk, I wouldn't think, *Those ladies are thieves!* But that's what I should have thought because that's exactly what they were. No, those White women didn't stomp in and make as much racket as the men did.

They didn't holler about all the nice things the Roosevelts had. They didn't team up and haul huge furniture out the front door. But they did steal boxes and bags full of stuff.

It was hard to tell what they'd stolen, except one of the women giggled a high-pitched giggle and held a necklace up in the air for the other ladies to ooh and aah over. A couple of men went back in with the ladies for a second trip inside, and they came walking out hunched over boxes that looked heavy. Was that the china the ladies didn't want the men using as target practice? I'd heard Mrs. Roosevelt brag about her china set. She'd told Mama the plates had a trace of gold around the edges. Hand-painted flowers, too. Mrs. Roosevelt used to be a maid for many years, and the family she worked for had given her hand-me-down plates as a gift when Mrs. Roosevelt was too old to work anymore.

Now those plates would probably be going back into some White lady's house. A thief's house. And the criminals would be eating off them.

Wednesday, June 1, 1921, 8:00 a.m.

I didn't know how in the world she managed it, but Livvie fell asleep. I glanced over at her to see what she was up to, and there she was, curled up on the floor, her mouth open, slobber coming out, and one arm wrapped around Minnie.

I guessed it made sense. She'd gotten her belly full; she hadn't slept well the night before, and now that she had the opportunity—Livvie took a nap.

For a moment, I was jealous. My little sister lived in her own world. While Mama and I were petrified by what was going on down the block, Livvie was giving Minnie a pretend bottle of milk and napping.

Mama grabbed onto my hand, and her fingers trembled. I tore my eyes from Livvie to see what Mama was looking at.

Now there were more cars and trucks on our street, cars and trucks that didn't belong in Greenwood. Different White men and women. And they had moved across the street to the Casons' house.

Probably Mr. and Mrs. Cason had seen what had happened at the Roosevelts'. Maybe they figured they could reason with the White folks. I didn't know what went through their minds. All I knew was that Mr. Cason, right that minute, was walking out his front door with his hands up in the air. Then he shouted at them. A nervous, troubled shout. "Here I am. Don't shoot." It sounded like his voice shook just like Mama's whole body.

I watched as Mr. Cason started to walk across his front yard. He was wearing a sleeveless T-shirt, which made his arms look thin. I knew Mr. Cason. He was a strong man. I'd seen him cut weeds with a scythe. His ropy arms swung the metal blade effortlessly, like it was nothing.

My eyes kept going back and forth. Mr. Cason. The White men standing in a clump. Mr. Cason wearing pants but barefoot. The White men with shoes on their feet and rifles in their hands. Mr. Cason's words quivering through the neighborhood. The group laughing.

What was so funny?

Mr. Cason stopped when he was in the middle of his yard, his arms suspended above his head. "Here I am. I'll come with you. Please don't shoot me," he said. One of the White men raised up his rifle easy-like, as if he was lifting up a cup of coffee to take a drink. My eyes went back to Mr. Cason. His whole body shivered.

The man racked his rifle.

"Don't shoot me, mister. Please," and those were the last words I heard coming out of Mr. Cason's mouth.

Poomb! In slow motion, Mr. Cason got shorter and shorter until he was on his knees. A dark circle in the middle of his T-shirt got bigger. Then, he was just a pile lying on the ground.

"Mama!" It was only a whisper but inside my head, I screamed.

She took my head and cradled it to shield me from the awful.

It was too late. Awful had already come to Greenwood and had shoved peaceful clear out of the way.

The group stepped over Mr. Cason's body like it was a heap of trash, as they headed into the house.

"Let's see what's worth hauling out of this place," one of the men shouted as they stomped and guffawed their way to more looting.

That was all Mama needed to see. We'd watched while the Roosevelts' house had gotten looted. We'd sat there while a neighbor got murdered right in front of us. I tried to imagine what was going through Mama's head.

We were going to be next. Maybe not exactly next. There were a few houses between ours and Mr. Cason's. And of course, there were the houses on the other side of the street. The little that I'd seen from these White thieves and murderers, the surer I was of one thing: these people wouldn't stop until everything in Greenwood that was worthwhile was stolen… and they'd kill any colored person they came upon—as long as it amused them.

If we didn't leave right away, we'd be the next ones looking at a rifle.

I stared into Mama's eyes. Surely, she'd have the answer, because I didn't know how we were going to manage to sneak out without at least one White man or one White woman seeing us, and once they saw us, they'd hunt us down like wild animals.

Mama's eyes were squinting so much, they were almost shut. There were deep furrows on her forehead. And her mouth? Her mouth was working double hard, as she chewed on her lower lip.

"We got to get out of here, Mama."

She shook her head. It looked like she was still searching for something.

"Mama! If we don't leave right now, they'll find us."

"If we leave now, they will find us. We got to do something to outsmart them." Her eyes darted around, still narrowed and squinty. Her eyebrows twitched. I almost felt like I was seeing the cogs turn in her brain.

She took me by both shoulders. Holding onto me with her strong hands, she said, "We're gonna hide. Here. It's the only way."

Here? In our house? We were going to hide while a bunch of White men traipsed around our home and while White ladies rooted around in our cabinets?

It was my forehead's turn to get all wrinkly. Mama and Daddy were so wise. They never did anything crazy, but this was a crazy plan.

"But Mama." I grabbed one of her hands. "They'll kill us."

"Not if they don't find us," and her mouth pursed up.

"We're gonna hide in a place where they're not gonna bother looking. And we're gonna be real quiet."

While we watched the Duprees' and the Hamptons' house get stripped of everything they'd worked years for, Mama told me her plan. "Those folks—they're looking for china cabinets and sofas and nice rugs. Tea sets and china sets. They won't even look twice at baseballs and bats." She smiled at me. It wasn't the kind of smile she had on her face when she and Daddy

114

danced in the kitchen to some song that only they heard. It was a sad smile.

My room? We were going to hide in my room? "In my closet?"

"No, that's not where I was thinking. They might know as soon as they see it's a boy's room that there's nothing valuable there. That doesn't mean they won't check the closets and obvious places to see if there's any colored folks hiding out."

She ran her hand along the top of my head and then scratched my scalp gently. "No, Henry, we're not gonna hide in your closet. We're gonna hide under your bed."

Wednesday, June 1, 1921, 8:30 a.m.

By this time, the looters had moved to the Berrys' house, the house across the street from our next-door neighbors. No longer was Mama holding a corner of the drapes open. Now we were completely silent and listening more than looking.

Apparently, it was time. Mama put her finger up to her lip, to shush me before I could even think to ask a question, as she pointed to the hall, towards my room. She put her hand over Livvie's mouth and kissed her cheek. Livvie rolled over as she woke up, whimpering, but Mama kept her hand clamped down.

She leaned over and whispered right into Livvie's ear. "We're gonna play hide and seek. As quiet as we can, we're gonna crawl into Henry's room. Let's go— the game's gonna start any minute."

Even though we weren't talking, we weren't completely silent. I was worried the sound of our knees shuffling across the floor would alert the looters, but they were still across the street, catty-corner from our house, getting really rowdy. They were laughing more, and shouting even nastier things about all the things the Berry family had.

Ida Berry took piano lessons. Just about every spring, summer, and fall afternoon most of the block could hear her practice, the notes floating from house to house. I'm sure those White men were surprised that colored folks had something as fine as a piano.

I hoped they'd get a hernia hauling that heavy piano out of there.

As soon as we got into my room, Mama had us sit on the floor in a circle. In a hushed voice, she said, "Olivia, there's a big game of hide and seek goin' on. Everybody in Greenwood's playing."

I had to hand it to my mother. What she said wasn't a complete lie. All us colored people were trying to hide, and all the White people were seeking to find us.

It was also clever because Livvie loved being the center of attention; she loved her baby doll Minnie, and she loved games. Hopscotch. Jacks. Tag. Jumping rope. If she thought there was a chance of her getting a prize, she'd bend over backwards and turn herself inside-out in order to win.

Mama grabbed my hand and one of Livvie's hands. We were a united circle. We were a smaller circle than we would have been if Daddy had been there, but that would change soon. Soon, Daddy would be back. Soon, either the White folks would succeed in getting Dick Rowland loose and they'd lynch him, or the sheriff would succeed in getting everybody—Black and White—to go home, and then Daddy would be home, too.

"I've searched every nook and cranny of the house, looking for the perfect hiding spot—and I've found it." Then Mama leaned down and whispered even quieter, like this was the biggest secret of them all. "We're going to hide under Henry's bed."

It wasn't the biggest secret. The biggest secret was what Mama and I had seen in the last hour or so. That was the secret I hoped Livvie would never have to hear or figure out.

She whispered more. "All three of us are going to squash in together. Once we get under Henry's bed, we can't move. We can't talk. We can't even sneeze or cough, or we'll lose the game."

"Oh Mama, that sounds like—"

"Sssh. Livvie, the game is almost ready to begin. Talk quick but talk quietly. The people who are the seekers are next door." My sister was so excited, the words burst out.

"This is gonna be so much fun," Livvie said, this time whispering.

"It will be fun. So much fun. But Liv, these seekers are going to try to scare us. They think if they make us frightened, we'll scream, and then they can find us." Mama pulled Livvie's hand up to her mouth and kissed it. "They're gonna stomp around and shout ugly things. They might even move our furniture around. They might break things. They'll probably check each room, but we're gonna be so quiet, they'll be able to hear a mouse pee on cotton."

Livvie giggled. Mama didn't say that too often, but whenever she did, it tickled my little sister.

"Do you think we can win this game? Henry?"

I nodded, even though I wasn't sure. I knew what the true parts were that Mama was saying, and I knew which parts were lies. I also knew how mean those White folks were. The men had been drinking. All night? They had gotten whipped up into a real frenzy between the Roosevelts' house and the Berrys'. If we gave those White people even the tiniest clue we were still there in the house, they'd rip up the floorboards and tear down the roof just to find us.

"Olivia?" Solemnly, like she was enlisting in the army, my little sister nodded her head. "If you need to relieve yourself, go now, but don't flush."

I didn't have to, but Livvie did, so I went with her and stood in the hall to remind her to be extra quiet.

Mama was on her hands and knees, next to my bed. "I think you should go first, Henry, and scoot until you're right next to the wall. Then you, Livvie. I'll get in there last," which is exactly what we did.

Lucky for us, my bed was a hand-me-down from Mama's sister, and the legs were spindly wood. It was old and looked it. There wasn't anything fancy about it, but it was tall. My mattress sat higher than Mama and Daddy's bed. In fact, there was so much room under my bed, Mama and I could lay on our sides and still have room to spare.

"If you feel yourself gettin' ready to sneeze or cough, put your hand over your mouth, hard, and stop yourself from making a sound," Mama said, so soft and quiet. When we got into our spots, I looked past Livvie and tried to look past Mama, but couldn't. Her head was right in my line of sight.

There was no way I wanted to be stuck in this dark place with people moving around who would shoot me if they had the chance, and all the while not able to see what was headed my way.

Sliding toward my headboard, on my side for a foot or so, I got in a spot I could see. Mama could see. I could see. Livvie was sandwiched between us like a slice of ham in-between two slices of bread. She couldn't see a thing, which was probably a good thing.

I stared at the edge of my sheet. It sure didn't go all the way to the floor, which meant it wasn't doing a very good job of hiding us. But as I thought about it, maybe that was a good thing. Maybe when they came in, the looters would figure that surely nobody was hiding under my bed because with so much space between the edge of my sheet and the floor, it looked like anything under my bed could be easily seen.

For a while, nothing happened. We still heard laughing and yelling at either the Berrys' house, or maybe they had finished across the street and were busy looting next door at the Staples' house.

The three of us were breathing so shallow and quiet, I was right there next to them, and I couldn't even tell there were two people jammed up against me.

Were we really that quiet? Or was it just my hopeful imagination at work? When one of those White men stepped into my room, would they hear us breathing in and out, so raspy and raggedy, they'd know right away there was somebody in here?

I tried to see my room the way the looters would see it. There was my chest of drawers. It was painted a light brown. It was sturdy, but had lots of dents, so the color it used to be showed through. It didn't seem like it was a piece of furniture that anybody would be eager to have. I was sure they'd seen nicer dressers in their looting.

There was my dirty clothes hamper. A basket full of sweaty boy's stuff? I didn't suppose that would lure them into stepping past the threshold.

Up against the wall, under my window, stood a small bookcase that was half full of paperback books and my collection of baseballs—baseballs that I'd found in the park. Most of them had some of the leather missing. Nothing of interest to a bunch of White grown-up men.

Except for my bed, that was it as far as furniture. There were some baseball player pictures thumbtacked to the wall. A framed picture of Grandma and Grandpa Simmons on top of my dresser. Propped up in a corner was my baseball bat, my mitt dangling from it.

Mama was right. At least I hoped she was right. Those men would take a couple of steps into my room, take a quick glance and figure they didn't need to bother looking any further.

"Let's see what these niggers got." It had begun. Livvie's game of hide and seek. Our game of life or death.

I heard Mama whisper, "Lord. Keep us safe." In my mind I added, *Please, Lord.*

They must have just flung the door open because we felt as well as heard the thud of the door as it hit the wall.

They might have been surprised it wasn't locked. When we went to bed, we usually didn't lock our doors. At night we felt safe. If we went shopping, we left our doors unbolted because our street, our neighborhood, was free of danger. Mama was right in saying no when I wanted to lock the bolt on the front door.

We'd seen for ourselves that locking the door wouldn't have kept them out. If they could just walk in and eventually leave, we might have some missing furniture or some missing plates, but our home would be okay.

Daddy was the one who kept us safe when we had to go into Tulsa. His strong shoulders, his walk of pride. When he walked down any street, whether it was in Greenwood or past the railroad tracks in White Tulsa, Daddy walked with confidence.

When he got home, he'd be proud we did something smart like decide to not lock up the house. Otherwise, Daddy would get stuck repairing a shattered window.

Bomh bomh bomh. They were foraging around where we'd been just moments ago.

"Eeew," Livvie whispered. She sounded thrilled. Livvie faced me. Mama faced out. Like me, she must have wanted to see what was happening past the underneath of my bed, but couldn't. Since it would have been almost impossible for Mama to reach behind her to keep my sister quiet, I did it.

I pressed my hand down onto her mouth and kept it there.

"Looky here." The voice was gravelly and slurred. What had caught their eye? Our sofa was old. Not valuable like antique old—old, as in Mama and Daddy must have gotten it before I was even born because that tan couch had been there for as long as I could remember. There were spots on the arms that showed how well-worn it was. It probably wasn't our sofa they were huddled around, and we sure didn't have a piano, so what was it?

Mentally, I walked around the rest of the room. There was Mama's rocking chair, but just about every house in Greenwood probably had a similar one. There was an upright wooden chair set up next to the end table, but neither one of those were worthy of a "looky here."

An anniversary clock sat on the mantle above the fireplace. It might have caught the looter's eye. The bottom part spun around, the brass looked gold, and it looked fancier than it was because Mama kept the glass dome over it clean, and I'd seen her, every week, she'd clean the dome and dust the clock before carefully putting the protective glass back in place.

It must be the clock.

"Look at these coloreds. Don't they look like they think they're high-falutin'? Like they think they're better than us?"

My eyes blinked a bunch of times, and my nose wrinkled. What people were they talking about? In my head, I went back, looking at what else was in our front room.

Then it hit me. They must have been talking about the family photos we had propped up on the mantle. There were framed pictures of my grandparents, both on the Robinson side and the Simmons side, but I didn't know why they'd called them high-falutin'. What did White people expect? Did they think Black folks should have posed hunched over, their knuckles dragging on the floor like they were monkeys?

My grandparents were proud people. They'd worked hard. Did my grandmas and grandpas think they were better than anyone? No, but they also didn't think they were less than anybody.

Bomb bomb bomb. It sounded like the looters were now in the kitchen.

There surely wasn't anything in there that would interest the men. A stove, a kitchen table that made even Mama sad every time she scrubbed a little more color off the top, wishing she could get a new one. Pots and pans hung up on the walls. Maybe the White women, when they got their turn, would be interested in rooting around Mama's kitchen, but the men couldn't have cared less.

Bomb bomb bomb. Bomb bomb bomb. Almost immediately, the thieves must have decided nothing was worthwhile in the kitchen, because the bootsteps got closer. In the hall?

It was obvious Livvie was excited. The expression on her face was a combination of sneaky-devilish-happy. Even though it was a bit dark, I could still see well enough, and I knew my sister well enough to know that she was biting on her lip to keep herself from grinning too big of a smile. She liked games, and she loved winning games so much that I felt pretty sure she was going to be quiet in order to win at this hide and seek game. At least I hoped so.

If only Livvie knew what our prize would be if we won. What would be our prize? Some furniture left in our house that they didn't steal?

I was glad she didn't know what the White people's prize would be if they found us and won.

Mama's back was to us. The back of her head was completely still. I had no idea what she was thinking or feeling. Livvie was facing me. Her heart beat wildly against my stomach. Probably my heart raced as well, the rhythm trapped by Livvie's head.

And the warmth that clouded around us—our quiet, shallow breaths hung there, like a fog. The closeness, the heat—it was on the verge of being suffocating.

"Lord, protect us," Mama whispered again, just loud enough for me to hear. In my mind, I asked God for the same thing too.

The sound of some piece of furniture, as it scraped across the floor or some furniture being bumped into ricocheted throughout the house. Were they in Mama and Daddy's room...or Livvie's?

"Harold! Look what I got!"

"What is that?" Their words sloshed back and forth between them, slurred and sloppy.

"What kind of high and mighty niggers live here?"

One night last year, a few days before Christmas, Daddy drank some buttered rum. He'd been at a bar with some friends from the garage where he worked. When he finally got home, he stumbled through the front door, talking funny.

"Hellooo, schweetie-pie." He leaned over, trying to give my mama a kiss, but missed. Like one of those toys that rolled around but never completely toppled over, he wobbled but righted himself.

Mama balled her hands on her hips and said, "James Henry Simmons, what have you been drinking?"

"Oh, just schum buttered rum."

"From what I see, I'd say you drank three buttered-rums past 'some,' James." When Daddy had been drunk, he was funny. After drinking all night, these White folks weren't silly. They were downright mean.

The sound of broken glass made me flinch. I didn't mean to jerk back, but I did. Then I remembered Livvie. I smiled a crooked smile, raised my eyebrows, and shrugged. She grinned back at me. It seemed my baby sister was better at this game than I was. Was she thinking that the seekers were making so much racket while us hiders were being awful quiet? Livvie knew. When you played hide and seek, if it was your turn to look, the more silent you were, the more likely you could catch a sneeze or a cough or a rustle from the hiders.

"Little glass horses? Little glass butterflies? Fancy little doodads on their dressers? These gorillas think they're better than White people." The sound of more broken glass, a rapid series of tinklings made me suck in my breath and hold it.

"Henry, why are they breaking my—" but I put my hand over her mouth to stop her whispering. It wasn't her fault, I knew. She couldn't help it. That moment, she had either figured out it wasn't really a game, or she'd realized that the folks who were playing hide and seek with us weren't playing fair. It was just like Mama had told her, but to have her figurines broken, well, Livvie hadn't been prepared for that. Never had my sister played a game where people broke things. You looked around. You searched. You didn't destroy things.

And my sister's glass collection was precious to her. She didn't have that many of those glass little things, less than a dozen I think, but in her mind, each one was special.

I clamped my hand over Livvie's mouth and did my best to hug her close to me without making any noise, as I moved in the cramped space.

"Them? Better than us? That's funny," one of the men shouted out. It sounded like he spit out the words.

Bomb bomb bomb. The stomping got closer. The wooden floor underneath us shook with each footstep. Could they hear us rising up and falling back down each time one of their boots hit the floor? Were they going into Mama and Daddy's room now?

As they moved around, stumbling and bumping into more things, I tried to see in my head what they were seeing in Mama and Daddy's bedroom. A rocking chair. It wasn't fancy, but it was good enough to hold Mama, as she rocked Livvie when my little sister was still in diapers and still drinking a bottle. Mama might have rocked me there too, but I was too young to remember. There was a bed, of course, but the bed was nothing special.

Their chest of drawers was a hand-me-down from Mama's past. I thought she had it when she was a kid. It was all chippy and looked old, but not the expensive antique kind of old. It just looked like the sad kind of old, like it had seen better days and had settled on being worn out.

There was a mirror on the wall by their closet, but because it had a big crack in the corner, the thieves probably wouldn't bother with it. Part of the silver stuff was peeling away, too.

Other than a rug that had been stepped on so many times for so many years, you could probably read a book through it, there wasn't anything that would interest these White men. At least I didn't think so.

"Lookee here. I should take it for my Elmerine." What was he talking about?

"Aww. Such pretty colors. I think I'll wear it the next time I go ballroom dancing," a different voice said. Several of them laughed. Usually I felt warm inside when people laughed, but when these men snorted and guffawed, my stomach tied itself into knots.

"Give it here. I saw it first. Elmerine's been wantin' a new bed covering. I think she'd fancy it."

"The price is right, that's for sure," said one of the men, and somebody snorted a loud snort.

Mama's quilt. The quilt that was too special to use on their bed. The one she hand-pieced out of scraps from Livvie's and my baby clothes. And of course the price was right. For people who steal, the price was always right.

The quilt was a mixture of brown and navy patches from my little boy pants and flowery patches from Livvie's little dresses. I didn't know too much about quilts and comforters, but I knew Mama loved that quilt. It was never spread out on Mama and Daddy's bed. Instead, it was folded up and draped over a quilt stand, which was probably why Livvie didn't grab it when she got all the other blankets and bed coverings. This quilt was more for decoration than warmth.

Did the man throw the quilt over his shoulders like a shawl? Had Mama figured out what they were talking about?

I couldn't tell. I tried to read her thoughts by looking at her back. Was she tensing up? Were her muscles getting all cramped and tight?

It was no use. Mama's back was a blank slate. She lay there on her side, perfectly still.

Bomh bomh bomh. Bomh bomh bomh. Now the wood planks shook like a giant was walking around. Each of their steps sounded like thunder. The noise bounced around, hit the walls, and angled down, so we felt as well as heard the men. I grabbed a hold of Livvie, held her tight up against me, and kept an eye on whatever I could see. They were here. In my room.

I saw Mama's head lift up off the floor. No longer was her cheek pressed against the floor of my room.

Worn-out boots. All of them were dirty and scuffed up. All I could see were the shoes and part of their pants.

"Anything in here?"

They shuffled and stomped around. I stared at the tiny clumps of dirt the men left, as they moved around.

"Nothin' but junk," another White man said, and then the sound of metal fast-scraping across something. What?

Something hit the floor. The tinkle of broken glass joined in with the sound of their shuffling. More broken glass. Shards flew across the floor. One piece skittered past the top of Mama's head. My cheek stopped it. The pain as the point slashed across my skin made me wince, but there wasn't room for me to stop the trickle of blood. It wasn't the time for that either.

"Yeah, just a bunch of kiddie junk."

Aaah-aah-ch-- Mid-sneeze, I covered my sister's mouth with the palm of my hand. The rest of me froze. That sneeze didn't give Livvie or me any warning. Sometimes, my sister had allergy problems. Of course, it happened today.

Mama froze, too. So did Liv.

"What was that?" At that moment, most of the White men were standing still, more or less. I could see some of their boots rocking, like they weren't too steady on their feet, but they'd stopped tromping around my room at the same time my sister sneezed.

"What was what?" another man said.

Please God, make them leave without finding us. And God, please bring Daddy back quick.

"I don't hear nothin'," one of them said.

Then, thankfully, somebody took a step and ground a piece of glass into the floor. It didn't sound like a sneeze, but it was a noise. To these White men who'd probably been drinking all night, it maybe sounded like the noise that had just flown out of Livvie's mouth.

More steps onto the shards of glass. "Yeah, I guess it's nothin'."

I saw Mama's shoulders, as they relaxed.

They left, taking with them the vibrations and any dirt that was still ground into the soles of their boots.

Mama's cheek lowered back down onto the floor.

"Let's get out of here. Nothing else worth gettin'," one of the men said. More clomping sounds made me think they left.

"Mama, we won the game, we—" Livvie whispered, but I covered her mouth with my hand again. I couldn't tell her, but the game was far from over.

"Ladies, it's your turn," one of the men shouted. It sounded like it came from outside. "Get your doo-dads and your pretties."

Barely loud enough for me to hear, Mama prayed again. "Lord, look over us."

"Ruth, look at this afghan. This colored's granny squares are almost as pretty as yours." These footsteps were quieter. Smaller shoes with little heels. This must have been the lady looters.

"Not even close to 'almost' as nice as mine, but I will take the afghan." Whatever woman it was, she giggled. "After all, I could use it to make a bed in the barn for ol' Rex." More footsteps. "I wouldn't dream of using an afghan for my family after it's been touched by the likes of them, but it would be okay for a dog."

No more afghan over the top of our sofa. I guess Mama would have to crochet another one.

More laughter that sounded like glasses tinkling up against each other. These White women didn't sound like they had been drinking, which made it even worse. Leastwise, that's the way I looked at it. These ladies acted like they were at a tea party, the way they carried on; when really, they were trespassing and stealing. They knew exactly what they were doing.

The group must have made their way into the kitchen because I heard cabinet doors opening and plates clattering together, as they were taken out.

"Oh, these are just old, chipped plates. Not even nice enough to put feed out for the chickens. These must have been some poor coloreds."

"Not as poor as they're about to be," one woman said. She must have found what she said funny because she let loose with a whole string of giggles.

They might have ventured into the hall, but it didn't sound like they even went into Mama and Daddy's room or Livvie's, either. They surely didn't come into my room. Probably they just peeked in. It was hard to tell. Their light footsteps didn't give much of a clue.

And why should they? Why should they have rooted around any of our bedrooms? After all, they'd been in other homes. From the looks of things, they'd had hours to shop and pick and choose, and these thieves were only bothering with what caught their fancy. Well-worn stuff wasn't going to interest them.

The click of their heels got softer and softer, and then there was no more sounds except for our shallow breathing. I listened for the door closing, but it seemed they hadn't bothered, they had just left our house wide open.

Wednesday, June 1, 1921, 9:05 a.m.

The three of us kept quiet for a while. From their shouts and laughter, I couldn't tell where they'd gone once they were finished with our house. Next door? Across the street?

"Stay here. Both of you. Don't move, and don't make a sound." Mama scooted out from under the bed and crawled out of my room.

Did Mama have to go to the bathroom? Was she sneaking a look to see where the White people were now? I didn't know why she'd left. I didn't know how long we'd been hiding, worried that each breath would be the one that gave us away. I also didn't know how long we'd have to wait until Daddy came home.

What were we going to do next? I imagined we'd first have to clean up the broken glass, otherwise the bottom of our feet would be bleeding like my cheek was.

We also had no choice but to look around and see what had been stolen and what was out of place. However, whatever was gone was not important. Daddy and Mama had taught me that things didn't matter. Things weren't important. What was important was God. Family. Friends.

A photograph that was now without a frame. A collection of pretty glass figurines. The loss of an afghan or a quilt. All those could be replaced or fixed. But the fires were awful. If downtown Greenwood was on fire, we'd have to keep watch over our house. We'd have to call the fire department if the flames started licking at the homes on our block. Other than that, what else could we do until Daddy came back home?

"Henry?" Livvie said it so softly, it was more breath than my name.

I shushed her as I pulled her closer to me. Soon we'd be out of this cramped space and could at least whisper, I was almost sure of it.

My right arm was dead. Spending all that time with most of it wedged underneath me had put it to sleep. It'd sure be good to be able to stretch out, stand up, and not be crammed up next to each other like we were in a tin of sardines.

The sound of knees and hands hitting the floor, one after another, was a welcome sound. Mama was back.

Mama's feet. Her legs. Her faded flowery dress. She crouched on the floor, peeked her head under my mattress, and said, "Come on out, but be quiet and stay low. It's not safe to show ourselves yet."

Livvie and I belly-crawled out from under my bed. We found out we didn't have to watch out for the broken glass on the floor. All of it—except for the piece that found me—had ended up around my chest of drawers. Mama's arms surrounded both of us as soon as we were able to kneel and straighten up our backs. Kneeling felt good after being stuck on my side for so long and being forced to stretch out my legs without bending them. Mama's embrace felt good, too.

Mama kept us in a circle and put her hands on our shoulders.

"Olivia, we've won the first round of the hide and seek game. They didn't hear us, and they didn't see us. That's wonderful. But this was the easy part. This was the inside-the-house part of the game." She smiled at Livvie but looked at me with serious eyes.

Play along, Henry. That's what I thought her eyes were telling me.

I whispered, "Liv, this is the most exciting part. You're gonna love the rest of the game." I couldn't say anything else. I had no idea where Mama was going with her lies.

Before this day, that was something my parents wouldn't budge on. Honesty was one of the four cornerstones of our family, along with love, faith, and integrity. I was told to tell the truth unless the truth would hurt someone's feelings.

There had been times when one of Mama's friends would come by the house to model a new hat or a new dress. "Don't you just love it?" they'd say.

Mama would say, "I sure do," and "Wherever did you get that?" But later, I'd hear her laugh with Daddy over the way her friend looked.

"She looked like a pigeon tryin' to be a peacock."

"That woman resembled a rhino that had just finished rolling in a field of flowers."

"Oh James, she looked like a clown with cleavage, tottering on high heels."

When I asked about it, they explained.

"If you're asked about something small, like how a pie tastes or how a lady is dressed and the truth will hurt their feelings, it's okay to tell a lie," said Mama.

Daddy added, "But if it's something big, something important, it's never okay to tell a lie, Henry."

The lies that Mama and I were telling Livvie were about the most important thing that had happened in our lives so far. It didn't get any more serious than getting hunted by a bunch of White people who hated Black people. But sometimes, I was learning, lies had to be told to keep people safe because sometimes, the truth was dangerous.

If we told Livvie the truth, it would hurt a lot more than her feelings. If I'd said, "Livvie, the White folks are stealing our stuff and burning businesses. If they find us, they'll probably kill us," she would have started screaming or bawling up a storm. And then they really *would* find us.

In a hushed tone, Mama said, "Livvie, your brother's right. The next part of the game is going to be played outside. We're going to have to walk a long time and hide in lots of places until the seekers give up. And then, we'll win the game."

For the first time, Mama noticed the bloody trail twisting and curving across my cheek. Up went her eyebrows, but we didn't have time to talk about how it had happened. Without even hesitating, she dabbed her thumb with her tongue and started cleaning off the blood with her spit.

In another time and another situation, I would have tried to twist out of her reach. Over the years, every time she did that, it made me cringe. I mean, having my mother clean off my face with her slobber?

But this morning? This morning I wasn't trying to get away from my mama's spittle. I just wanted these strangers to go back to their part of Tulsa, so we could get back to living our lives in peace.

"Henry, get your black sweater, gray sweater, and your black suit jacket. All of us need to use the toilet before we leave, but don't flush it. We don't want anyone to hear us or see us, so hunch over or crawl. We'll leave in a few minutes."

I ruffled my hand through my closet until I found my black suit. Why did Mama want me to get it? It barely fit anymore. The last time I wore it, I had to keep my arms plastered at my sides. If I'd moved my arms at all, the whole back would have split right down the middle.

And my sweaters? I dug them out of my dresser. Why did she want them? It was the first day of June. It wasn't hot now, but it was certainly going to be warm later in the day. Definitely not sweater weather.

However, I wasn't going to ask any questions. Today was a day where I was just going to do as I was told. Any questions would have to wait.

Wednesday, June 1, 1921, 9:15 a.m.

Mama grabbed my sweaters and jacket. Draped over her arm was what looked like Daddy's suit jacket. Were we going to meet Daddy somewhere, and he needed to be dressed up? Still, I squashed down my questions. I figured I'd find out the answers in dribs and drabs. Why we needed sweaters and jackets right now wasn't important. Getting somewhere safe and getting back with Daddy was the most important thing right now.

"We're gonna stay off the street. If we sneak through the backyards, we got a better chance of winning this game of hide and seek," Mama told us.

My sister couldn't keep her excitement from bubbling out. "Oh Mama, you mean we're gonna hide behind bushes and—"

"Sssh. We have to be quiet still. Yes, we're going to walk when we can, and sometimes we're going to stop and hide in flower beds and behind trees." Mama tucked some of Livvie's hair behind her ear. Usually, she plaited my sister's hair in the morning. That was part of their every-morning routine, but this morning was not like every other morning. This morning, if I had looked out the window and saw grass up in the air and clouds at my feet, it would have gone right along with all the other strange things that had happened.

"Liv, we won the first part of the game. Do you think we can do just as well on this next part?"

Livvie grinned and nodded in small, quick movements. At that moment, I wished I was a little kid again without a clue about what was *really* going on.

Mama said, "I think so, too. Since the game has started up again, we need to leave now. The quicker we can find a good hiding spot, the better our chances," and Mama cracked open the back door.

We crouched behind her, as she listened first, then stuck out just her head, looking. Gripping onto the door frame with one hand for support, she leaned out. Mama was crouching close to the floor, so if any White people were looking for colored people still in the neighborhood, they probably wouldn't see Mama huddled down by the ground. They were looking for people who were five feet tall. Six feet tall. They weren't looking for people who were as tall as a small dog.

Mama turned and looked at me. "Henry, you left the wagon by the flower garden?"

I had gotten used to listening closely to words that weren't much louder than a gentle breeze. Whispering had become a normal way of talking. I nodded.

"Well, that's where we're going then. Follow me, but let's walk like ducks. Like this," and in the middle of the kitchen, she bent down, so she was halfway crouching and half hunch-backed while she walked. Her rear end was sticking out, just like a duck's tail feathers.

Part of a grin turned up one side of my mouth. My sister giggled. Mama rubbed my shoulder; she touched Livvie on the cheek and then peeked out the back door one last time.

"Let's go."

Livvie went out right next to Mama. She tried her best to walk like a duck; but really, my little sister was short enough, she didn't need to crouch down too low. She already was close enough to the ground to be invisible. At least, I hoped she would be invisible to any White people still on the lookout for Black people.

Every sound made it seem like I was watching a movie instead of living the moment right then. It was like I watched it happen to me, instead of living it.

I heard shouting somewhere down the street. It was too far away to hear exactly what they were saying. They sounded like White voices, and there was a strange echo that made the words bounce around the neighborhood.

The whole street was empty. It sounded like all the other families, except for us, were gone. There weren't any mothers or fathers or packs of children to soak up the sounds.

The birds hadn't left. Their chirping told me their homes had not been rooted and rifled through. Their homes were still in fine shape.

As I looked to my left and my right, over and over in the short trip to our flower garden, I didn't see anything moving—only us.

The still-smoky smell that drifted towards us reminded me of what Eunice said, that Greenwood was getting burned down.

Above us, clouds of black and gray smoke twined themselves together in the sky. Some rose up in narrow columns, and some formed fat and billowy shapes from the ground all the way to the sky.

When we burned leaves, it was one of the smells that reminded me autumn had arrived. It was a smell I loved. It meant the trees were turning beautiful colors and that snow was around the corner. When Daddy barbecued, my mouth watered and my stomach gurgled, but this smoke wasn't a smell that made me feel good inside. These clouds didn't mean something fun or delicious was waiting for us.

No, this smoke meant that things were getting destroyed.

We crouched our way to Mama's garden. There, next to the rose bushes and the mums, was our wagon. The red paint that hadn't been worn off over the years blended in with the flowers, making it almost look like a patch of red geraniums. Squatting next to the wagon, Mama pulled us next to her, so we were all hunkered down together.

Mama said, "Livvie, you're the lucky one. You're going to start out in the wagon." Mama spread out the blankets to make a cushiony mattress. She picked up Daddy's thermos, the sack of leftover biscuits and her bag and set them down on the ground.

What was in the bag? I was curious, but this was just another question that I'd add to the string of curiosities. Later. Later, I'd either discover the answer when she opened up the bag, or I'd have to ask.

My sister's lower lip started to stick out, and I thought I knew what she was thinking. Whenever she suspected she was being treated like a baby, she turned into a mule—uncooperative and stubborn.

"You'll be pulled along like you're a queen. Princess Olivia. I wish someone was hauling me around like I was royalty." I knew all-too-well what made my sister pout and what made her puff up like a proud bluebird. Getting something extra, something that nobody else got, was something Livvie couldn't resist.

It worked. Her eyes darted around. Was she imagining the wagon was a carriage, and Mama and I were going to take turns being her horse?

Mama said, "You even have room to lie down, Liv. You might be tired. None of us got much sleep last night." She put her arm across my sister's back and gave her a hug. "Let's get you settled in," and Mama patted the bed she'd just got finished making.

Once Livvie was lying down in the wagon, flat on her back, Mama took my sweaters and folded them up into a pillow. Raising up Livvie's head, she slipped it underneath. My jacket and Daddy's jacket were folded and rolled and slid onto either side between my sister and the wagon.

That answered one of my questions. By the time those jackets were pulled out of the wagon, they'd be creased in all the wrong places. Clearly Mama wasn't thinking Daddy would need to be dressing up anytime soon. My mother was quite particular about many things when it came to the cleanliness of our home, our appearance, and the way we carried ourselves. There was no way Mama would let Daddy wear something that had wrinkles crisscrossing every which way. There must be some other reason for the jackets.

Leaning over, Mama said, "Your job is to protect our water and our provisions." She filled in the other empty places in the wagon with the thermos and the biscuits. "You can also keep an eye on the sky, Olivia. The people who are seeking us are sending smoke signals to each other. It'll be your job to see if you can tell what they're saying. Do you think that's something you could do, Liv?"

Of course my sister ate it up like it was Mama's peach cobbler swimming in a pool of fresh cream. She nodded slightly, her mouth set in a serious straight line, her eyebrows raised just a bit.

Mama grabbed her bag and the handle of the wagon. We were off.

Wednesday, June 1, 1921, 9:30 a.m.

The yards on our street and in most of the neighborhood were fairly flat, which was a good thing. We didn't need any hills as we dragged along Princess Olivia.

Our old wagon didn't make much noise, as we made our way across our yard and into the Staples'. Daddy had kept the axles and the steering column oiled up, even if it was just a kid's toy. Anything that had wheels, anything that had working parts was well taken care of by Daddy.

Mama and I stayed low and kept a sharp eye out. We moved in the direction the looters had already left. They'd gotten what they wanted and had moved on.

Bump-bump-bump. Mama's arm was stretched behind her, like it was part of the handle. As we passed by the Staples' house, past their tomato patch and their geraniums, I looked.

Not a soul to be seen. The back door was wide open. Maybe the White thieves had looked in the backyard for bikes or lawn mowers?

The smell of smoke filled the air. Somewhere close—the next block? Two blocks away? Clouds and columns of wispy gray met in the sky so that it was impossible to tell where one fire ended and the next one began.

I didn't look up much. One, I didn't want to think about what places were burning. Eunice's words kept coming back into my head.

"They're burning down Greenwood."

I figured the White people were burning down the stores. The theaters. The library. They wanted to wreck our neighborhood; there was no question about that. If we didn't have places to shop, if we didn't have any banks, life would be rough for us colored folks.

Would they burn down the churches? That one got me thinking. I mean, wasn't there just one God for everybody, whether they were Black or White? Would the White folks risk getting God angry at them?

Or were they so mad about Dick Rowland and so hungry to hang him, they didn't care?

I also didn't look up much because I needed to keep my eyes on the ground. In the beginning, Mama was pulling Livvie. She had enough to worry about, what with dragging the wagon along behind her and her bag looped over her shoulder. If I kept paying attention to the sky instead of where I was going, I'd probably trip and fall. Mama didn't need to start pulling two kids.

Besides the smoke that filled the sky, there wasn't much to look at, as we walked through the backyards. Nobody was playing catch, like they usually were during warm mornings. No dogs were tied up and barking or running until they ran out of rope. No ladies were digging in their flower beds. Far off (I hoped it was far off), I heard gunshots.

When there were some bushes bunched up together, Mama had us stop, crouch down, and she'd peek around the edges of the bush to try and see what was going on.

After she did it a few times and after watching where Mama looked, I figured out what she was doing. She tried to pick bushes or flower beds that were on the corner of a yard, so she could look between the houses and see the street. With us walking behind the houses and across yards, we had no idea what was going on in the street. Certainly, Mama was happy we were able to travel without being seen. I started looking where Mama was looking. At the next few stops, there was nothing to see except a deserted street. Empty of all life.

But then we heard shouting. We squatted down in the next bunch of bushes. Livvie had fallen asleep, the bumping of the wagon a lullaby.

"Get on. Move!" Just three little words, but those three words were packed with meanness.

I hugged Mama as I got into a spot where I could see, too. What was going on? Who was getting yelled at?

If I'd been watching it in the theater, I'd think it was a string of criminals being walked to jail because there were colored people shuffling along in a single-file line, their hands up in the air, and none of them were talking.

Most of them had their eyes wide open, the white parts showing, like they were ready to bolt.

These weren't criminals. They were people I knew or had seen grocery shopping or in the park. I'd seen them working in their yards. I'd seen them in the movie theater. Mrs. Tate. Mr. Kimbrough. Mr. Grier. Mrs. Mackley.

"You're too slow, nigger," someone said, someone I couldn't see, I heard the sound of metal sliding on metal. *Crack!* A gunshot, so close to where we were hiding.

"Oh, Jesus!" a woman screamed.

In slow motion, one of the men opened his mouth wide in horror. Or surprise. Or pain. His head tilted back as if his neck was no longer attached to his shoulders. His face turned a little towards us, and I could see who it was. It was Mr. Curry, the owner of the grocery store.

Lord God, don't let him die here. Let that just be a warning shot. I know him, Lord. He's a nice—

Like it was a dream, Mr. Curry started to disappear. Farther and farther back he tilted, until he fell completely backwards onto the street, a flat heap.

"Oh, Mama," I said. My breath was ragged, and my voice was louder than it should have been, but I couldn't help it.

"Sssh." She tried to shush me, tried to keep me quiet, but it came out more like she was comforting me. Putting her arm around me, she hugged me, pulling me closer to her.

Without even thinking about it, I cupped my hand around Livvie's shoulder, careful not to wake her up. Me, Mama and Livvie. All connected, like beads on an unbreakable string. Soon Daddy would be back to join us, and the Simmons string would be complete.

The horror of Mr. Curry played out slowly, like time had frozen and then advanced, one second at a time. Some women cried. That metal sliding along metal sound. Again. A man cackled.

Time then ticked away at its normal speed. Some White man kicked the grocer, who didn't move, and the man said, "Move too slow and the same thing will happen to you." The group moved down the street and out of our sight.

I shuddered. The little bit of breakfast I'd eaten swirled around, causing tiny tidal waves to form. As the oatmeal hit the sides of my stomach, back and forth, all of a sudden, I knew.

I knew I was going to be sick. Yanking myself out of Mama's embrace, I leaned over, and everything gushed out. The only real noise it made was when the vomit splashed onto the ground.

"Henry, sweetie," Mama whispered. She rubbed my back. If we had been at home, she'd have gotten a cool, wet rag to wipe my face. But we weren't home.

Maybe there wouldn't even be a home to go back to? Maybe the fires had spread, and our house would be burning soon?

I wiped my mouth with the back of my hand. My stomach felt better now that it was empty, but my brain kept playing the grocer getting shot, over and over.

"Henry. We gotta keep going. I'm sorry." Mama moved until her face was right in front of mine. I could see the tiny flecks of gold in her eyes.

She kissed me on the forehead.

We walked for a while. I took the wagon handle from Mama to get Mr. Curry off my mind. Doing something physical—doing work hard enough to make a person sweat—was a cure for lots of things. That's something Daddy said.

If Daddy were here, he'd have helped make sense out of what I'd seen. Or at least make it make as much sense as possible. Since Daddy wasn't back yet, I tried to imagine what he'd say.

"Son, I know it's tough to see a man murdered right in front of you, but there are evil, ignorant people—people who just look at a person's skin color and hate them just because of that."

Daddy would have probably shaken his head right about then.

"We can't judge them, but the law can. And if the law chooses not to, there's always God."

I could see Daddy nodding slowly and solemnly after that bit.

"The one thing we can be happy about: Mr. Curry was an honest, kind man. He lived a life full of virtue. He's going to go to Heaven, no doubt about that."

Daddy would most likely smile. He wasn't the most religious person. Sometimes Mama would have to poke him with her elbow in the middle of the sermon because Daddy had fallen asleep. He wasn't the best churchgoer, but he did believe that when a life was over, reward and judgement would be dispensed.

Just imagining what Daddy might have said made me feel a little better.

The neighborhood gradually changed colors. No longer were the houses all cream-colored and white and pale green.

Now there were blocks that were a sea of black and gray.

It didn't look like the fire had spread from the shops to the streets with homes because I couldn't see a burned trail leading from the business section of Greenwood to any of the houses. Not all the houses had burned down. Here and there, a house stood that was still untouched.

A few houses up was one of those still-standing homes. I looked over at Mama. She had her eyes glued to that tan-colored house, like me. Maybe, like me, looking at all that charcoal and burned-up furniture made her sad.

Something moved. Ahead of us, two men were walking up the street. In uniforms. Mama and I froze.

They were walking in the same direction as the three of us. We could only see them for a few seconds because of the angle we had.

Their uniforms were blue. "Mama. Those are policemen. They're coming to hel—"

Tight as a vice, Mama clamped her hand over my mouth.

I was so excited, I'd forgotten. I needed to be quiet. There were police just ahead, just a couple of doors away, but if any of the looters were roaming around, they might get to us before the officers could stop them.

Seeing the police stopped the thoughts that were spinning around in my head. We'd seen a flood of people running through the neighborhood, scared to death. We'd seen houses get broken into and things stolen. We'd seen a line of law-abiding people marched down the street, like they were bank robbers.

We'd seen two men we knew shot to death.

Now we were safe. They were White policemen, true, but they'd stop anybody else from stealing from the colored families because stealing was a crime.

I smiled at Mama. For the first time since I woke up in the middle of the night to the sound of gunshots, there was finally going to be someone to stop the horrible.

Then I frowned, and my eyebrows scrunched down, making wrinkles on my forehead. I couldn't understand it—Mama didn't smile back.

"What about this one?" one of the policemen said.

"Yeah, why not."

What were they talking about? This one? This one what?

Mama pointed to a flower garden thick with azaleas and daisies. As silently as we could, we moved towards the corner of the yard until we were hidden. We could see the tan house, but we were hoping nobody could see us.

"You got any matches? I'm all out."

"I got an extra book. Here."

Matches? I looked at Mama, my eyes as round as baseballs. Mama, a sad look on her face, nodded. I shifted closer to Mama, and when I did, I stepped on a small branch, and it snapped. Loudly.

One of the police officers had rounded the corner of the tan house and was on the side. He had a stout stick in his hand. When the branch cracked in two under my feet, the policeman immediately stopped in his tracks and tilted his head to one side.

"What was that, Harry? Did you hear it?"

"Naw. What did it sound like?" the other officer called out. Was he checking to see if any people were still hiding in the house?

The policeman we could see stood there, listening. I froze. Mama froze. Livvie woke up, stretched and tried to sit up. Mama cradled Livvie's head. Even my breathing got shallower while Mama hunched over and rubbed Livvie's tummy to keep her calm. I made sure my feet didn't move even an inch.

The officer with the stick then shook his head. "It was probably nothin'. Some rodent or something."

He threw a rock through the side window, lit a match, then set one end of the stick he was carrying on fire.

It must not have been just a stick from the way the fire instantly blossomed. It must have been a torch. Tossing it into the house, he yelled, "Whoo-eee!"

My mouth dropped open. The torch must have hit the curtains because hungry flames licked out of the window right away.

I glanced again at Mama, trying to make sense of what I'd just seen, but Mama was no help. She refused to look at me. She just kept staring at the tan house that was now on fire.

Another storm swirled in my belly except this time, there wasn't anything to come up. I leaned over and tried to throw up. My stomach heaved. A bit of spit but nothing else.

Mama rubbed my back again, but it seemed like she was just doing it out of habit because her eyes were still stuck on the tan house, and her hand wasn't really rubbing, it was more like feathers moving across my back.

"Mama," I said, so soft I wondered if she even heard me since she didn't turn my way. "Mama, why did those police officers set that house on fire? Aren't they supposed to save us, protect us?"

It was only then that Mama looked at me. A tear trickled its way down her cheek. "Henry, nobody's gonna protect us anymore. "

Seeing two people killed right in front of me and seeing Mama cry frightened me. We still hadn't met up with Daddy. We still weren't in a safe spot. My mother used to be a tough, strong mama. I was wondering if that had all come to an end.

Was it because it was only Mama now? Was it because Mama didn't have Daddy to help hold her up? We had no idea when these horrible things would come to an end, which made me wonder if I'd have to step up into both Mama and Daddy's shoes until Daddy found us, or we found him.

It was no fun seeing Mama crumple and start to crack. No fun at all.

Now we were in a sea of black and ashy gray. No more houses standing. No color except for blackness and all kinds of shades of gray for as far as I could see.

Livvie was fussing, even though we did our best to keep her quiet.

"Mama, why is the sky so gray? It smells bad. And where's Daddy? He's been gone a long time."

I wanted to tell her it wasn't just the sky over our heads that was gray. The air we were breathing was gray, too. It was almost like I could taste the air. The stuff I sucked into my nose and my mouth tasted like I was in the middle of a fireplace and was eating the burned-up firewood. I wanted to tell her I wondered the same thing: where was Daddy? But I didn't.

Livvie started coughing. Mama told her to hold Daddy's work thermos, and when she felt a cough coming on, she should take a sip of water.

It was strange to see what was floating in the sky. Bits of ash floated in front of our faces and rose and fell before disappearing. Some of it almost looked like tiny scraps of charred paper, but I figured that wasn't the case. We'd done enough science experiments at school for me to know that when paper burned, it didn't end up in small sheets like this. This stuff that was fluttering around in the breeze probably came from the houses that had burned down. I didn't need to wonder what diaries and letters were floating in the sky. Whatever families had accumulated over the years had gone up in a blaze in a single day.

It wasn't just Livvie and me. The smoky air was giving Mama a hard time. Whether she was pulling the wagon or whether she was taking her turn and walking with just her bag over her shoulder, I could tell Mama was breathing heavier than before. She huffed and puffed. It was easy to hear her take in air and then let it out noisily.

Not noisily enough to draw attention to us. Just enough sound for us to hear.

When it came to color, the three of us blended in fairly well. Mama's dress was covered with tiny black flowers. I had on navy blue pants and a white shirt. Livvie was only visible when she sat up. Most of the time, she was happy to lie down like she was the Queen of Sheba, so she didn't stand out. None of us were a beacon to the White people who roamed around, looking for colored people to lock up, and that made me relieved.

I didn't exactly know what the White men were doing with all the people from Greenwood. When I saw them walking along the street, looking like a line of criminals with their hands up and a gun pointed at them, I figured it wasn't a good place they were being forced to go to. I figured if someone—even someone White—had told them, "We're going to take you to a place where you can find your missing family members, a place where you'll be safe, a place where you can get all your questions answered," it wouldn't take a gun to get them there. They'd happily go. They'd probably run to wherever they were told to go.

Of course if they had been heading to a good place, they'd have no reason to put their arms up like they were being arrested.

They couldn't all be going to the jail because it wasn't that big. Mama and I had seen dozens and dozens of people marched to who-knows-where, and that was only in the part of Greenwood where we were. The three of us were traveling through a small part of town. It made sense that when we were on corners that we couldn't see around and on blocks we didn't hide behind, the same thing was happening. I had no idea how many colored people were being forced to march down the streets. Nor did I know where they were going.

I just knew it wasn't the jail because even if they were stacked up like firewood, all of them wouldn't fit.

I also knew that as bad as we had it right now, it was a whole sight better than the unknown the marching folks had to deal with.

My arm no longer felt like it was part of the wagon handle. No longer did it feel like my arm was metal that just made the wagon handle longer. When I took my turn pulling, my arm was more rubber than metal. Using up as little energy as possible and still pull Livvie or still keep walking was all I could do.

Who knew how long we were going to have to walk? Who knew where we were headed?

I didn't ask Mama. We didn't talk much, except when Mama would see something I didn't, and she'd quickly whisper, "Let's hide over there," as she pointed. Or I'd spy something, nod in the direction, and simply say, "Mama!" so she could weigh out the situation and decide what we should do.

I was glad. I didn't want to hear any lies from Mama. The ones she told Livvie—the ones I'd joined in on—were enough. The little lies Mama told my sister, telling her this was a big game of hide and seek, that people were doing it for fun, that they were trying to win—well, those last two might have been the truth. I wasn't sure if they did it out of meanness or because they thought it was fun. The stealing, the terrorizing, the killing. What made people do that?

That they wanted to win? That wasn't a lie, but all Livvie figured was there'd be a prize at the end for the winner.

The problem? I knew what the prize was. I knew that if all the colored folks could be put into jail cells and pens, after all our homes were cleaned out and burned down, these White folks would consider themselves victorious.

There was one thing Mama told us, without even saying it out loud, and I didn't want to wonder if it was a lie or whether it was the truth.

In fact, I kept Mama's unspoken promise in the back of my head and the center of my heart, and I refused to speak about it. If that promise stayed in a safe place, then soon…

Well, soon, what Mama promised would come true. At least I hoped so.

But here was where I finally found out why Mama had wanted us to bring along my sweaters, my black suit jacket, and Daddy's suit jacket.

We blended in fairly well, but fairly well wasn't good enough for Mama. She wanted to make sure we didn't end up marching down the street like all the other folks we had seen being driven to who-knows-where.

Because we were surrounded by burned-up homes, from Mama's perspective, even my navy blue pants and her flowery dress and our red wagon made us a little too visible.

Since there were no more houses to hide behind and not many gardens or bushes, we had to camouflage ourselves. The first time it happened, I knew better than to say anything. I just did what I was told.

Mama draped Daddy's jacket over the side of the wagon, so it was black instead of red. She and I huddled under one of my sweaters. The other sweater was tossed on top of Livvie.

The first time it happened, Mama whispered what she was going to do ahead of time.

"Liv, it's more of our hide and seek game. You've been doing so good, and now you're going to get to hide under one of Henry's sweaters. Be as quiet and as still as you can; otherwise they'll find us, and we'll lose the game."

I had to hand it to my sister. She had been extra good. Not a chatterbox like she usually was. Not asking a never-ending string of questions. Most of the time she was happy to lie in the wagon and get dragged around. We'd had a couple of pieces of biscuit now and then, along with tiny sips of water from Daddy's thermos. And of course, there'd be times when we had to relieve ourselves. Being a boy, I had an easier time than Mama and Livvie, but I'd just turn my back and wait for Mama to tell me I could turn back around, to give them as much privacy as I could.

The way Liv smiled when Mama told her how well she'd been playing so far told me my sister still thought we were in the middle of a game, and she was bent on winning.

When she found out it was all a lie, would she be mad? Or disappointed? I wasn't sure.

It seemed like once all of Greenwood was burned down, the White folks left. I guessed they figured there was no need for them to hang around in our neighborhood anymore. No more mischief for them to do. There was nothing else to destroy. No more people to round up, to torment, to kill. By this time, I was sure all the colored folks were somewhere else. Where, I didn't know. I just knew we hadn't seen any other Black people in a long while.

It was just me, Mama, and Livvie in a sea of charcoal gray.

We got to the edge of Greenwood, finally, and had a choice of roads. The three of us stood there, surrounded by a few tall sycamores and some overgrown weeds and rested for a moment.

Mama looked to the right and said, "That road goes east." I knew enough about directions to know that if we took the road headed east, we'd be walking right smack dab into White Tulsa, and that would not be a good idea.

Then Mama faced to the left. "That road goes west." Because I ran the neighborhood, I knew that Greenwood was west of the White section of Tulsa. Did we want to walk into the business section to gawk at the stores and businesses that were now just piles of bricks and burned wood?

No. If we didn't see all of our neighborhood burned to ash, maybe we could pretend that somehow pockets of Greenwood had survived.

"This road straight ahead goes north." Mama turned her face up to the sky. She was still whispering more than talking, even though there was nobody around us, at least nobody I saw. She arched her back, like she was surrendering to the heavens or to someone who was looking down on us. "James Henry Simmons, wherever you are right now, you'd better keep an eye on us. Give us some guidance." She sighed, a loud one, kneeled down, hugged Livvie, then stood back up and hugged me. Her thin but strong arms sent a river of love into my heart.

"We're going north. Daddy will know that if Greenwood's gone, we'd head north, so he'll go north to find us." As we started our journey again, a warmth spread inside of me. Mama talked to Daddy just like I did? It was like she knew he was somewhere in Greenwood, and our prayers and requests would travel on the breezes to find him, wherever he was.

We headed north. North like the escaping slaves headed, towards an unknown land, towards freedom, towards a better life.

I was hoping our unknown destination would be a welcoming one. I hoped that wherever we went would be free of people determined to exterminate us. I surely hoped that wherever we were going, we'd find peace.

And Daddy. Most of all, I hoped wherever we went, we'd find Daddy soon.

Thursday, June 2, 1921, morning

We got mighty tired of walking. We'd been walking for more than a day. Sometimes, Mama pulled Livvie, and other times, I'd drag the wagon behind me. It was like we didn't have to speak to each other to know when one of us had almost reached the point where we couldn't go any farther. I'd reach over for the wagon handle, and Mama would let her hand drop. I tried not to let her know how worn out I was. I didn't complain because what good would it have done? The three of us were in this boat together, surrounded by an ocean of hate and sadness.

There were even times when Livvie got so antsy, we'd let her walk for a while. That meant we made slow progress with my sister toddling along next to us.

So the three of us walked and walked. Or rather most of the time, two of us walked and one of us rolled. Oh, there were more times when Livvie wanted to get out of the wagon and walk than we'd allow. She'd squawk a little, but most of the time, Mama shushed her up right away by making a game out of it.

"Sweetie pie, why are you fussing? You're in a chariot! Me and your brother are your horses. Just sit back, relax, and enjoy the ride." That would shut her up. I'd look back and see her grinning like she was some Roman princess.

There was no way we would have made any headway with Livvie toddling between us for most of the journey. We were walking as fast as possible, taking breaks now and then to rest a bit or get a drink of water from somewhere. Our thermos of water—Mama treated it like gold. Whenever Livvie whined about being thirsty, Mama'd say, "We'll get a drink in just a few minutes," knowing good and well my little sister would forget about it for a while if she didn't get what she wanted right away.

I understood. Mama did, too. There was no use for any of us complaining about being on the road and headed to who-knows-where. We probably had no home to go back to. There was no reason to whine about how dirty or how tired we were. Everything we had—except for our wagon and whatever was in Mama's bag—was now most likely black and charred. The only thing my baby sister could complain about were the things she needed right now. She was hungry; she was tired; she needed to pee; she was thirsty.

We all were.

We were so exhausted; it was a miracle we were able to continue putting one foot in front of the other. Mama and I took turns pulling the wagon, but she never lowered the loopy handles of her bag to leave it behind or even to start dragging it along the ground-- even though it was extra weight to carry.

What in the world was in that bag? I wanted to ask. I did. It almost came out of my mouth too many times to count. Talking about Mama's bag meant I'd be able to take my mind off all the awfulness that had happened yesterday.

I tried to figure out what was in the bag by looking at the shapes that made it bulge out here and there. It looked like there was something square-shaped and something larger that could be a picture or painting. The bag didn't seem like it weighed a lot, but walking as long as we had, anything extra was a burden.

There must be some reason why Mama kept what was in the bag a secret.

As we plodded along, when we heard the rumble and bump of a car, we'd veer off into the ditch. If we heard lots of loud laughing and voices that sounded like they were drunk, we'd get off the road even faster. If we passed by a field, we'd head into the brush. If the covering was thick enough, we'd also relieve ourselves while we were there. If we could hear a creek close by, we'd head that way, and we'd all cup our hands and get a drink, and Mama would refill Daddy's thermos. A few times we walked deep into the woods, found a spot that would keep us hidden, and we curled up and took a nap. I think Mama even got a few minutes of sleep, although I think while we napped, she mostly kept a sharp eye on Livvie and me.

We had to travel like this. It wasn't like there were restaurants and gas stations lining the road with welcome signs. "Come on in, colored folks, and rest a spell."

Nobody held out welcoming hands to help us. We were on our own. It was just the three of us—without Daddy.

Thursday, June 2, 1921, 1:15 p.m.

My sister kept us sometimes talking about normal things. "Mama, what kind of bird is that?" I heard the same sound. *Weet weet weet churr-churr-churr-churr-churr.*

"I have no idea, Liv." As she kept glancing around, I knew she wasn't looking for birds. "What kind of bird do you think it is?" Mama's voice broke in the middle, like it took all her energy to just keep the conversation going.

My sister sat up straighter. Even though I was worn out, it tickled me. Little kids were so funny. It didn't take much to get them excited.

"I think maybe it's one of those bright blue birds. You know the ones I'm talking about?"

All Mama did was give her a "hmm hmm" as she pulled the wagon behind her.

When we got to the top of a small hill, we saw a house. The paint on it had seen better days, but the yard was well-kept. From what I could see, it was a yard that would make Mama proud—flowers here and there and some bushes that obviously got regular care.

Then something moved in the yard and made me quickly look at the ground and keep my eyes focused on the road and hope I could pass by unnoticed. There was a White lady doing something in her front yard. Mama must have had the same idea and started pulling the wagon faster, so we could get past the woman before she saw us.

Our plan didn't work.

The White lady called out. "Ma'am?"

The sound of our feet moving fast along the road, in unison, filled my ears. Mama acted like she hadn't heard. Being colored meant we got great at pretending. All the time, we had to pretend it didn't hurt our feelings when White folks insulted us and pretend they had the right to do that. We had to pretend like the unfairness that was heaped on us was completely fair. Too many times to count, we'd had to swallow our anger, instead of letting it loose.

She got louder.

"Ma'am?" Her voice was full of questioning. It wasn't mean or sounding like she was going to accuse us of anything, just louder. Mama slowed down just a bit. I did too, so I could still be side-by-side with her.

"Ma'am? Do you live in Greenwood?"

That question made Mama skid to a stop. The wagon handle clanged into the back of her legs. I glanced over. Tears came to her eyes and started streaming down her cheeks.

I leaned over and put my arm around her waist.

The White lady stepped closer to the edge of the road, close enough so that she was able to see my mother's tears because the stranger's eyes narrowed up and turned down, like she was feeling sorry for my mama.

"I'm sorry. I meant did you just leave Greenwood? Are you heading north?" The White lady halfway bent down and smoothed down her dress around her knees, as a welcome breeze fluttered up her hem a bit.

"Yes, ma'am." I could barely hear Mama. Her head was down. Was she embarrassed about her crying?

"Have the three of you been walking the whole way?" For the first time, the lady looked at Livvie, and she smiled at my sister. And I knew just what Livvie would do once the White woman smiled at her because my sister lived her whole life like she was the center of the universe. Livvie cocked her head to the side, showed off her dimples, and gave the White lady her best smile in return.

"Yes, ma'am." Mama looked up and held the woman's gaze for a few seconds. I knew my mama well enough to notice her warming up a little. She wasn't looking as scared as she was a minute earlier. The skin around her mouth stopped looking so tight. Her frown lines almost disappeared. She dabbed her tears dry with her fingertips.

"Yes, we've been walking for more than a day now."

"A whole day? You must be plumb worn out. Thirsty and hungry too, I imagine." She waved one arm toward the house. "I've had a pot of beans cooking all day—too much for Merrill and me to eat. Would you like to sit down and have a bite to eat?"

My mouth fell open. I couldn't help it. When I did that in public, Mama would fuss and say, "Are you a fly-catcher? Close your mouth!"

But this was something new. We weren't allowed to eat in Tulsa restaurants with White folks, and in Greenwood, everyone was Black. Never had I been offered food by a White person. If Mama said yes, I had a whole new set of questions that would keep my mouth looking like a bug-catcher for quite a while.

Would we eat at the same table with this lady?

Would we eat off her nice china, or would she give us our beans in battered old pie tins?

What would we drink from? Would we get real glasses or cups to sip from, or would we have to hunch under the pump and drink from the stream of water that came out? I'd never encountered anybody White who would like having a glass or cup in their cupboard that had once had the lips of a colored person on it.

I figured probably she was nice enough to give us some food, but we'd have to eat in the backyard, like the chickens or the family dog.

"That would surely be nice, if it wouldn't trouble you too much." Mama was saying yes? I couldn't believe it.

"You three would be doing me a favor." The lady chuckled. "There's such a mess of beans in that pot. Merrill and me will be eating them until Christmas if we don't get some help." She crouched down and asked Livvie, "How 'bout it? Would you help me get rid of some beans and cornbread?"

Lucky for Liv, she remembered her manners. "We sure would. Thank you, Miz Lady."

That made the woman chuckle again. "I guess if we're going to sit down and eat together, we should be able to call each other by our names. Otherwise, how can I get you—young lady—to pass the cornbread when I want another piece?" She paused as she straightened up. "I'm Miz Ruth."

Mama said, "I'm Miz Margaret. This is Henry and Olivia." No mention of Daddy. No mention even of our last name.

"Let's head on in, so I can check on those beans. Even though I'm complaining about how they seem to have multiplied while they've been simmering, I sure don't want 'em to burn," and again, she gestured towards the house.

I followed Mama's lead. We bumped the wagon across the yard to the front porch, a little behind Miz Ruth. When we got to the porch, Mama stopped. By that time, Miz Ruth was at her door and getting ready to open it. She turned around when I guess she didn't sense us right next to her.

"Ma'am. We'd be glad to sit on the edge of your porch and have a bite, if that's okay with you." Mama stood ramrod straight, but her head was slightly bowed. Once she stopped talking, she stared right at the White lady. Tiny twitches were going on in the corner of Mama's eyes. Nerves? Tiredness? I wasn't sure.

I could see Miz Ruth's eyes move around, looking like they were making a journey around Mama's face. "Nonsense. These porch boards are so rough, they'll likely give you splinters. Come on in, where you'll be more comfortable."

Mama looked at me, her face as blank as a clean piece of paper. I had no idea what was going on in her head. She reached down and helped Livvie out of the wagon.

As we followed her like a line of ants towards a crumb, I wondered, *Was she just being hospitable, or was she worried what her neighbors might think if they saw three colored folks setting up residence on her porch?* Again I wasn't sure, but I hadn't been sure of anything for the past couple days.

The front room was both cool darkness and warm brightness. Parts of the parlor were shady, hiding from the sun. Because the curtains were flimsy and flittered in the breeze, there were patches of light that danced across the floor.

"Let's settle in the kitchen, and I can get you all something to drink. Walking all that time, I know you got parched." She pulled out a chair for Livvie and waved a hand at the other chairs. "Sit down. Give your feet a rest."

Pulling a pitcher of lemonade out of the ice box. Miz Ruth then got four glasses. "I know water is the best thirst-quencher, but sometimes, we just need something with a little sugar. Olivia? How about a sweet drink?"

My little sister again remembered her manners. "Please, ma'am. And thank you." She looked at Mama.

I figured it was my little sister making sure it was okay to accept a drink from this White stranger, although Miz Ruth didn't seem like any other White person I'd ever encountered. Out of the corner of my eye, I saw Mama nod. Liv was doing just fine.

I tried not to be too obvious, but I was too curious not to sneak some glances. What did a White person's kitchen look like? Their hair was different. Their skin was different. It just might be that everything about them was different.

The little I could see? Our homes were pretty much the same with just little differences. Mama hung her pots and pans on the wall from nails. Miz Ruth must have kept hers in the cupboards. Mama's salt and pepper shakers were a rooster and a chicken. On the table where we sat, there were two little flowers in flowerpot-things that must have been the salt and pepper. This table had six chairs set around it. Our table only had four.

Sneaking some more looks, something all of a sudden punched me in the stomach. Our kitchens were nothing alike—probably not now. The last time I saw it, our home was fine. But now? Now it was probably just a pile of charred and burned-up wood and ash. The salt and pepper shakers Mama wiped clean every day, the pots and pans she scrubbed each time she used them, the chairs she carefully arranged after each meal was over—they were ruined, burnt, destroyed. What had being particular and proud gotten Mama? The homey things she fussed over were most likely all gone. We had a wagon, a couple of blankets, and the mystery stuff in Mama's bag. There was probably nothing else left of the Simmons family as far as things.

It was my turn to cry, but only a tear trickled down before I sniffled, and Mama looked at me, as I pretended I might be coming down with a summer cold. But Mama had been studying me for the past twelve years, and she knew everything about me by heart. Reaching across the table, she grabbed my hand and held it for a minute.

She squeezed my hand, and I knew her well too. She was saying, *Maybe later there'd be time for tears. Not now.*

For the next half hour, we worked our way through beans, collard greens and cornbread. I would have liked a second helping, but when Mama caught me eyeing the cast iron pan of cornbread, still half-full, she gave me her evil eye look. Miz Ruth must have read my mind because she spooned the last of the greens onto my plate, along with the pot liquor, my favorite.

"There's just a little bit left, not even a helping, Henry. Would you mind finishing it up?"

"Thank you, Miz Ruth." I couldn't help smiling.

Mama had lost that round. I'd gotten more to eat

and there was no way I could have said no because this White woman didn't ask first. She just plopped it onto my plate. Besides, if I put up a fuss and told her I wasn't supposed to have a second helping, that Mama had just got done slicing me up with her eyes over my wanting more, that would have insulted Miz Ruth. Mama and Daddy both impressed on me many times that if I could avoid it, I shouldn't hurt someone's feelings.

I remembered once Daddy had gotten a plate of cookies from Mrs. Thomas. He'd fixed her car on a Saturday in front of her house. It didn't take much time, but she was appreciative.

When she dropped off the cookies, my sister and I both homed in on them right away. They were pretty, decorated with different-colored sprinkles. Mrs. Thomas stepped inside for a moment, insisting my daddy have a cookie right then and there.

"I baked 'em special for you, James. I know what a sweet tooth you have. Just have one now, while I'm here. I want to see your face when you taste it."

He picked up a cookie, admired it like it was a piece of art, and took a bite. "Um-um, Miz Thomas. These are mighty tasty cookies. You didn't have to, but thanks."

Later, Daddy told us while we were eating dinner, "She said I had a sweet tooth? Well, I almost had a broken-off tooth. That cookie was harder than a brickbat."

Yes, I'd been taught to be careful when it came to people's feelings.

Would I ever again get to laugh at the little messes Daddy got tangled up with? Or would there be no more lessons he taught, just by his example? This time I squashed down my sorrow before it could rise up and brim over my eyelids. There'd be time later for crying. I was sure of it.

Not much talking while we ate. I did my best to keep watch over Livvie and made sure she didn't knock anything over, made sure she didn't put her elbows on the table, made sure she didn't slob anything on herself or onto Miz Ruth's floor. Miz Ruth seemed to understand that we just needed a safe place to be quiet and fill our bellies up before we continued our journey.

"We surely appreciate this, Miz Ruth. After a meal like that, I think we can walk clear to Canada before we're hungry again." Mama carefully put her knife, fork, and spoon onto her plate and half-rose out of her chair. "It was delicious and filling. Could I help clear the table and do the dishes before we're on our way?" This was another time my mouth hung open so wide, a whole swarm of flies most likely started doing figure-8s over my tongue and around my teeth. Mama working with—not for—a White lady to neaten up the White lady's kitchen? I couldn't wait to see this.

"How about you stay where you are for just a minute? It won't take long to get things cleared off and start the dishes soaking."

I guess Mama thought the least she could do to thank this lady for feeding us was to follow her directions because she nodded and settled back onto her chair. Once the dishes were covered with soapy bubbles, Miz Ruth sat down again. She raised her eyebrows, her mouth twisted into a half-smile, half-frown, and she looked at each one of us.

"Miz Margaret, I don't think you three should be leaving right away. It'd be better if you stay the night, get your strength back, get a good night of sleep." She lightly drummed her fingers on the table and looked up at the ceiling, like she was searching for something.

"That's kind of you, but feeding us did a world of good. We've been getting some shut-eye along the way in short spells. We're no longer thirsty, and our stomachs are so full, we're stuffed to the gills. We can't impose on you any further, ma'am."

Miz Ruth shook her head slightly and pursed her lips. "It isn't safe yet. I've seen several truckloads of those KKKers going up and down the road in both directions. Their fun in Greenwood is over, so now they're lookin' for more trouble. If they happened upon the three of you, they'd..." her voice dropped off, as she looked at Livvie and me.

Did she really think we needed to be protected from hearing what hate-filled White people would do to us? Really?

We'd lived through more awful in the last two days than I would have ever imagined. We'd seen White people do things I didn't think a human would ever do to another one. What could we hear that would be worse than what we'd already lived through and seen?

"I've got some cots down in our basement. Merrill built 'em. They're not pretty to look at, but they're sure sturdy. You should stay tonight, maybe a couple of nights, til things die down. And before you say anything, it's no imposition. It's just as easy for me to fill the pot all the way with some extra beans and fatback than it is to only fill it halfway." She nodded at Mama and smiled. "At least, come downstairs and look."

Mama glanced at me. I glanced at her. I wasn't sure what she was thinking, but I was thinking what if Miz Ruth is no different than the White folks in Tulsa?

What if all this lady wants is to shove us down in her basement and keep us there? And her husband, Mr. Merrill. What about him? Maybe he'd be mad about having a few colored people spending the night in his house. Oh sure, she'd bent over backwards to be nice to us, but maybe it was all a trick. Maybe she—

Mama put her hand on my shoulder and said, "We'd be glad to consider your invitation, Miz Ruth." Mama nodded at me and closed both of her eyes for a moment. Even as she nodded her head gently, just enough for me to see, I could tell she was more tired and full of sadness than I'd ever seen her.

Mama was our rock. Oh sure, Daddy was the big strong one. He was the one who went out every day and worked to keep us fed. When heavy things needed to be lifted, he was the one who did it. When I was younger than Livvie is now, I cut my foot on a piece of glass. It was Daddy who carried me into the house, acting like I was light as a loaf of bread. Daddy was the one with strong muscles, but Mama was the one with the strong heart.

She gave me a worn-out smile. Again, nobody but me would have figured it was a smile.

Like a family of ducklings following the mama duck, Livvie and I got right behind Mama, and Mama was right behind Miz Ruth, and we all headed down the stairs.

They were steep and narrow. The stairwell was almost completely dark, except for a patch of light coming from somewhere past the steps.

And the smell. It smelled cool. It smelled cool and old. I can't explain it any better than that. The air that came up and met us, as we walked down to meet it, was much cooler than the air in the rooms we had just left and cooler than outside.

My eyes took a moment to adjust, so I just stood there at the bottom, holding Livvie's hand, waiting. Waiting to see what Mama did.

A noise came from the far corner of the basement and cut right into my being. Something or someone was scuttling around.

In other words, we were not alone.

Thursday, June 2, 1921, 2:30 p.m.

Mama stopped following Miz Ruth, stiffened up, and backed up until she was pressed up in front of Livvie and me, like a shield. Her back was as straight as a broomstick.

"Oh, Mr. and Mrs. Jefferson. Deborah. Here are the folks I told you I'd seen on the road."

From the shadows of the corner came a colored man and woman and a young girl. I guess she was their daughter, but I wasn't for sure.

These folks looked tired. Tired and worried. Both the man and the woman had bags under their eyes. Their shoulders slumped, like they'd carried a heavy load of worry on their backs.

And they didn't look us in the eye. Their gazes went straight to the floor. Were they ashamed of something? Were they embarrassed?

For some reason, I didn't think it was either. I saw them glance up at us a few times. I recognized the kind of look they gave us.

In Greenwood, there were a couple of boys who were mean as snakes. They loved nothing better than cornering a wild rabbit and scaring it half to death.

Mr. and Mrs. Jefferson had that same look. A frightened look. A we're-surrounded-and -might-have-to-run-for-our-lives-any-minute look.

Miz Ruth reached out her hand and gestured towards the three strangers. "Miz Margaret, Henry and Olivia, these are the Jeffersons, and their daughter Deborah." She adjusted the strap of her apron. She nodded at us. "I'd seen you three walking when I was looking out the window. I went downstairs and told the Jeffersons they might have some company. That is, if we could convince you folks to spend the night."

Mr. Jefferson nodded at Mama. His wife started to reach out, then she pulled her arms back to her sides and said, "Howdy, Miz Margaret." Had she been about to hug Mama?

Mama turned, so she faced each person briefly. "I should have fully introduced us earlier. We're the Simmons. My husband James—" and Mama's voice faded to nothing.

Miz Ruth matched Mama's look, made a sympathetic hmmm, and then said to us, "I saw the Jeffersons on the road, just like you folks, a few hours ago. I figured they needed a place to lay their head for a day or two. I gave them a bite to eat, and when I saw they could barely lift up their spoon, I figured they needed to sleep a bit, so they headed down to the basement."

Looking at Mama, Mr. Jefferson said, "Ma'am, we rushed out of town when they were dragging people out of their homes and walking them down the street, like they'd committed a crime. Made 'em put their hands up like they were marching 'em to jail." He shook his head. "We didn't figure that was going to come to a good end for those folks. We didn't want to end up the same way, so we took our chances on the road."

Mrs. Jefferson looked at each of us, one at a time, searching our faces for something. I don't know what she was looking for. She looked like she was about to cry. That, I understood.

I'd been on the edge of crying a bunch of times since the whole Dick Rowland mess had snowballed into people dying and homes getting destroyed. Would I want my friends to know? Would I want Franklin and Carl to see me cry? No. It was okay to cry when I had been Livvie's age, but now? Boys who were twelve and still cried got teased. But I wondered how many boys my age were crying in Greenwood right now? How many men?

Mrs. Jefferson's eyes got rounder and wetter. I didn't know if she'd found what she'd been looking for when she examined us so carefully, but at least she'd gotten brave enough to say something besides howdy.

"We had no idea where we were headed. We just wanted to get out of Greenwood." She had her hands clasped in front of herself and twisted them around, like she was wringing out a dishrag.

Her husband put an arm around her shoulder and said, "We were lucky. We got out of town still alive. Then we got even luckier. We passed by Miz Ruth's house, she saw us, and flagged us down."

"I don't know if it was luck." Miz Ruth's voice trailed off.

That made the hairs on my arm stand up at attention. She said it like there was a whole lot she was leaving out.

Who wouldn't consider it good fortune or luck? A colored family escaping a city on fire and then getting helped by a White lady? A White lady feeding and eating with a colored family, especially considering what kind of meanness the White folks in Greenwood had dished up for us? Why would Miz Ruth doubt that it was luck?

Was this like one of those scary movies? I remember seeing the movie *The Werewolf*. There was a part I still remembered because it had made me jump out of my seat.

At one point in the movie, a woman was walking around in her house. Well, it was more of a castle than a house. She didn't know it, but everybody in the audience did: there was a werewolf hiding in her cellar.

Anyway, she was walking around and across the bottom of the screen, her thoughts appeared. "I don't know if I should go and check on the cellar. It's so dark down there," and when she said that, spooky music started playing.

Miz Ruth saying she didn't know if it was luck made me think there might be something lurking behind her words. Maybe she planned on luring us downstairs and—well, I didn't know what she might have been plotting.

But if it was all a scheme to do something horrible to us, it certainly was a good one. Feeding us and being so nice to us meant Mama and I had dropped some of our worry about being around Miz Ruth. Some. Not all.

Of course, Livvie was too young to be suspicious. She just tagged along behind us, happy for anything that came along.

Miz Ruth walked deeper into the basement and pointed to one end. "We don't have the basement divided up. But there's plenty of room." She pointed to the other end. "There's a spot at both ends for each of your families to have some privacy." Then she chuckled a quiet chuckle. "Merrill made a dozen cots a while back. He didn't have a clue what motivated him to get the wood and draw up the plans and spend a whole day sawing and nailing. He said it was like a voice was telling him to do it."

She looked at the six of us. "Isn't that strange?"

We all nodded. In my head, I was saying, *Miz Ruth, you don't know even half of the strange we've seen. We woke up in the middle of the night to no Daddy. Planes were flying low around Greenwood, doing who-knows-what? We've seen a couple of people shot dead for no reason at all. We've seen policemen set a house on fire. We've probably lost our house. Your husband making a bunch of cots? Not even close to the amount of strange we've seen in the last day or so.* But I sure didn't say it out loud.

If I'd opened my mouth and said what I was thinking, Mama would have thought it was being disrespectful, along with being impudent. A few years ago, Mama had raised her hand, about to slap me in the mouth and said I was getting close to being impudent. I didn't remember what I'd said to make her so angry, but I had to look the word up in our family dictionary. I read that impudent meant rude. Saucy. Fresh.

If I had said what was swirling around in my head, I doubted Mama would have slapped me there in front of a crowd of strangers, but later she'd tear into me with her mouth, and my mama's words could hurt a whole lot more than a hand across my face.

Miz Ruth took a deep breath. She shifted from foot to foot a couple of times. "Why don't I leave you folks to get acquainted with each other, and perhaps you and your family will then agree to spend a night or two here,

Mrs. Simmons? Would that be alright?" We looked at the Jeffersons. They looked at us. We all turned back to Miz Ruth and nodded.

The White lady turned and headed up the stairs. "I'll be upstairs if you need anything."

As soon as we heard Miz Ruth's footsteps over our head, Mama sighed. "Mr. Jefferson, Mrs. Jefferson, are you going to stay here? Do you feel like it would be a safe thing to do?" She tilted her head from one side to another.

Mr. Jefferson said, "We'd talked about it." He looked down at his wife, a question on his face. I saw Miz Jefferson give him a little nod. "I guess we'll spend at least tonight here. We don't have much choice. Deborah twisted her ankle, and she can't walk too well right now. We figured, a day or two to get the swelling down and get her back in good shape—then we can be on our way."

He put his hands out, his shoulders scrunched up, and he half-smiled, half-frowned. "Is it safe? I surely don't know, but at this point I'm worn out. I can't do nothin' else except rest a bit and see what's in store for us next."

Mama stared a hole into the basement floor. Didn't say a thing. I looked down too, figuring whatever answer she'd find there, I'd see it too.

The floor was rough. It had seen better days. There were places where it was pockmarked, like little pieces had been dug out.

Taking slow, deep breaths, Mama finally looked up, but she didn't focus on the Jeffersons. Instead, she stared off at something above everybody's head, towards the corner, and whatever she was looking at, it seemed like it was far away.

I held tightly onto Livvie's hand. Again, I tried to see what Mama was seeing.

Nothing was there. The spot she was concentrating on was just a dusty corner of the basement.

I closed my eyes. Maybe Mama had her own magic she was trying to conjure up. Maybe she was looking for God, for some guidance from Jesus Christ.

I opened my eyes. The only one I thought could give me answers appeared.

I shivered. My mouth went slack. There was Daddy. There, in an old pair of work pants and short-sleeved, gray-checked shirt—the same clothes he'd been wearing the last time I saw him—stood my father.

"Daddy. What should we do?"

He had big bags under his eyes. His forehead was full of worry-wrinkles. His brown eyes stared right into mine, like they were flashlights. And then he spoke.

"Henry, there are times when strong people stand up and fight. You and your mama and Liv stayed home and fought for your lives. There are times when folks run. You three were smart. You ran when it was no longer safe to stay in the house."

Daddy's shoulders sagged. That wasn't like him. Daddy always stood tall and proud, the way he told me men should always carry themselves.

"And there are times when you just stay put. Lick your wounds. Give yourself time to get better."

Daddy's right hand reached out and grabbed my shoulder. His fingers spread out, held my whole shoulder in his one hand. His fingers lingered there. "This is one of those times. Stay here."

He still looked at me. But as we stared at each other, his eyes changed. They went from bright and full of love to dull. Like they weren't Daddy's eyes anymore. I searched, but didn't see any feeling in his brown eyes.

"Stay here…'cause there's nothing left for you in Greenwood."

"But that's not true. Daddy, you're still—"

And then he faded away. When he had come to me, he'd appeared instantly. One minute, there was nothing in front of me. The next, he was standing there.

But when he left, he left gradually. In pieces. His grip on my arm loosened. Then, I could see through him. It was like he was painted onto a thin piece of gauze with watercolor paints. Finally, he disappeared in wisps, like someone had taken a paintbrush and erased bits of him, here and there, with swipes of the brush.

"Daddy! Come back!"

Mama's head swiveled in my direction. She gasped, and one of her hands flew to her chest. I realized that time, I'd spoken out loud. The rest of the conversation between Daddy and me had been in my head, I guessed. But it had seemed so real, and when Daddy disappeared, I couldn't help but cry out.

"Henry!" she whispered in an attempt to shush me. She shook her head at me with such tiny movements that only I could see.

"This is what I wonder. What's in store for us? When we go back, what will Greenwood look like?" Mama said and stood behind my sister and me, encircling us with her arms.

Mr. Jefferson opened his mouth, looked like he was going to speak, but then was silent, like he had changed his mind. Either that, or he rethought what he was going to say. His lips twisted grimly to one side. After a moment, he said, "Miz Simmons, I think Greenwood is gone. I don't think there's anything left." He stared down at his hands. "When we left, houses were ablaze—on purpose. The whole neighborhood was being cleared out. Planes were dropping down kerosene bombs." He looked at Mama, then me. "If they were bombing us, they didn't mean to leave anything standing." He looked back down at his hands. We barely heard him as he said, "I'm sorry if what I said made your hope drain out. For me, ma'am, all hope is gone."

Mama matched his softness when she said, "For me too."

For a while, our family and the Jeffersons talked. It was strange. We talked about everything except all the horrible things we'd seen. We talked about Deborah's music lessons (violin) and baseball. We talked about the kind of summer we were supposed to have (cool, with lots of rain). Mama and Mrs. Jefferson talked about the hairstyles the girls were begging for.

We stood, all bunched up, and got to know each other. I didn't talk, and neither did Deborah. Livvie just kept staring at Deborah.

Deborah was between Livvie and me, age-wise. She was nine. I had seen her at school, but since she was younger than me, I didn't pay her any attention when I saw her on the playground. She seemed nice enough, here, but I didn't have much choice. Right then and there, if I decided I didn't like her, the next day or two would be miserable.

It would be like having another little sister. For me, one was enough.

If anybody was listening to all of us, they would have thought we were friends standing on the sidewalk, gabbing away. No way would they have thought we had just met and were going to spend the night together in a stranger's basement. No way. The way we were chatting with each other, people would have thought we'd been long-time neighbors, but I wasn't even listening. I was thinking about what Mama had said to Mr. Jefferson.

Mama's hope was gone? Hope for what? Hope for our house? Or did it go deeper? Did Mama no longer think that Daddy—

No! My head and my heart were not going to go down that path.

Thankfully, my worries got interrupted. "How are y'all doing?" Miz Ruth's voice came down the stairs and reached us before she did.

When she made it all the way down the steps and was standing by us, Mr. Jefferson said to her, "Just fine, ma'am."

She smiled. It looked like a real smile to me. Maybe she wasn't going to turn into something evil like a werewolf or a vampire. Maybe she was just a nice White lady. However, I hadn't ever seen a White lady who was kind. I'd only seen mean ones, so if that's what she was—a nice one—then it was another first for me.

"Mrs. Simmons? Have you decided? Are the three of you going to stay here and rest up a bit?" Miz Ruth tilted her head a bit to one side. When she did that, she looked like a bird watching the grass for signs of a worm. Her brown eyes were bright and full of curiosity. The complete opposite of Daddy's eyes right before he vanished.

Mama bowed her head in Miz Ruth's direction and said, "We'd appreciate a night or two of your hospitality, Miz Ruth, if it wouldn't inconvenience you too much."

Miz Ruth smiled. "Not at all, not at all. Cooking for just Merrill and me is hard. I love to make big batches of things." She laughed. "The trouble is I make a big batch of rolls, and they get hard before we can eat them up. I make a big batch of soup, and by the time the soup is done, we're tired of it."

"I wish I had that trouble." Mama cupped her hand around my cheek and under my chin. "With a boy like Henry, along with my husband James, I hardly ever get any leftovers to worry about. Sometimes I think this boy has two hollow legs."

Miz Ruth's arms went out, like she was about to encircle us with an embrace. I took half a step back—couldn't help myself. White hands reaching out in a nice way?

"Why don't we go upstairs? Merrill should be home soon, and in the meantime, we can figure out what we're having for dinner." The six of us colored folks swiveled our heads around, looking at each other. Livvie's eyes zeroed in on Deborah. She probably wasn't even listening to what everyone had said. I got it. If it was a boy around my age who was with the Jeffersons instead of a little girl, I would have been sizing him up and ignoring everybody else.

What real choice did we have? We all followed the White lady up the steps.

When we got into the kitchen, Miz Ruth stood by the sink, her hands clasped in front of her.

We stood too. Us colored folks? There were six chairs around the table, but we hadn't been invited to sit down. Even if we had been, we still might have stood. If we all sat, cooling our heels while a White lady stood up, would that have been right?

That would never happen. At least, it could never have happened in our heads. We couldn't have imagined it.

I'd never been in the same restaurant with White people before, but I could tell what kind of attitude they had when I was in a store in the White part of Tulsa. Even if White people came into the store after us, even if they got in line behind us, they still got all huffy and expected to get waited on before us. And they did get waited on first. Since they acted like they were more important than us, I figured the same thing would have happened here in this lady's kitchen. If she was standing, we all should stand—unless she told us different.

I was holding onto Livvie's hand when I felt her bouncing. I looked down. She was shifting from one foot to another, fast, over and over.

Leaning down, I whispered. "Why are you doing that, Livvie?" I tried to keep my impatience out of my voice. Livvie had been so quiet since we'd gotten here, she hadn't caused a lick of trouble.

Livvie answered in the loudest whisper I'd ever heard, "Henry, I have to pee."

That was a problem. On our trip, after we left Greenwood, we held it until we were out of town, and then we stopped along the side of the road. Tall weeds, bushes, trees crowded up together. Those were all perfect spots to stop.

Okay, maybe they weren't perfect places to empty our bladder and our bowels, but they were the best we were going to get along a road we were unfamiliar with as we headed to a place we had no knowledge of.

Mama heard her. In fact, probably everybody in whatever town this was heard Livvie pleading to pee. She was that loud.

There was no point in Mama asking Livvie to hold it. Hold it for how long? Until tomorrow? Until the day after tomorrow?

The problem was in Greenwood, we could use any bathroom we wanted. If we had dinner at a diner in Greenwood, we could use the bathroom there. Shopping in a Greenwood store after drinking too much water? Not a problem.

However, once we crossed the railroad tracks to the White side of Tulsa, it was a different story. We weren't allowed to use the same bathroom that White people used. On the Tulsa side, there were signs reminding us. Colored water fountain. Colored bathroom. If we were somewhere, had to use it, and we weren't close to a colored bathroom, we just had to hold it.

For me, it wasn't a big deal. It was something I did automatically without thinking of it.

But it was a big deal. Apparently, it was a huge deal because people had been killed, and houses had been burned down, all because Dick Rowland couldn't use the bathroom in the building where he shined shoes, so he had to go across the street and into the elevator, and then I don't know what happened. All I know is a lot of mess could have been avoided if everybody could use whatever bathroom was closest.

It *had* been a while. We'd stopped to relieve ourselves right before we rounded the curve in the road by Miz Ruth's house, but since then we'd eaten, and I didn't watch Livvie to see how many glasses of lemonade she drank. She was probably ready to either pop or puddle.

I glanced at Mama. She pushed a few stray hairs out of her face, the space at the top of her nose wrinkled up, then she cleared her throat.

"Miz Ruth, we're going to step outside and head down the road a little ways. We'll be back momentarily—if that's alright with you."

One of Miz Ruth's eyebrows arched up. The other one hunched down. She squinted—just one eye. "I don't understand. Why do you want to leave?"

Mama took in a deep breath and then let it out slowly. "Ma'am, we don't want to leave. We need to leave. My little girl needs to use the toilet." She ran her hand down Livvie's cheek. "I'll take her down the road a bit, we'll find a spot, out of the way, and we'll come back. That is if it's okay."

Tap tap tap. Livvie's pee-pee dance was speeding up.

Miz Ruth said, "But why would you leave? I have a bathroom right off the hall." She shook her head a little back and forth, like maybe she was confused.

Mama looked down at her feet.

Tap tap tap tap tap. Livvie really needed to go. "Here. Let me show you where it is," and light as a feather, Miz Ruth touched Mama's arm. Without another word, Mama and Livvie headed out of the kitchen, right behind Miz Ruth.

The rest of us looked at each other, bug-eyed. It was clear the Jeffersons had been holding it since they had been invited in. I figured they were thinking the same thing I was thinking. This was one strange place.

First of all, no White folks had ever touched us with gentleness. Ever. In fact, most White folks did everything they could to avoid touching colored people. Sometimes they stepped off the sidewalk and into the street to avoid getting close to us. I'd seen colored folks in Tulsa get pushed or elbowed, and the White people doing it would have a snarl on their face. They didn't even try to act like it was an accident, so to see someone in my family touched with White kindness, when all I'd ever known was White meanness—well, it made my eyes threaten to pop out of their sockets.

Secondly, we'd never had permission to use the same toilet a White person used. To sit down on the same seat. To use their toilet paper. To wash with the same soap they used to wash their hands. This was another reason that my eyes bulged.

Apparently Miz Ruth considered it normal because she came right back after showing Mama and Livvie where the bathroom was. Before they returned, Miz Ruth told the rest of us that she was thinking about making a chicken casserole. "I got some fresh chicken, and we can put it with some rice. How does that sound to you folks?"

She scanned all our faces. It wasn't up to me to answer. I was just a kid.

Mr. and Mrs. Jefferson both answered at the same time. One of them said, "That sounds just fine," and the other said, "That'd be wonderful."

Miz Ruth started getting things out of her cupboard, scurrying around the kitchen. She turned around and saw we were still standing there, our arms kind of hanging at our sides, not sure what to do.

"Oh my goodness, where are my manners! Have a seat, Mr. Jefferson, Deborah, Henry. Sit, please," as she waved her arm towards the kitchen table. "Mrs. Jefferson, I wonder if you'd mind helping. I figure we need a lot of rice to feed all these hungry folks—Merrill included, when he manages to get home." Mrs.

191

Jefferson walked over, stood next to Miz Ruth and before our very eyes, those two ladies started working together as a team. Miz Ruth would ask Mrs. Jefferson to get something off a particular shelf, or she'd ask her to do something, and side-by-side, they worked.

When Mama returned, Miz Ruth showed us all where the bathroom was. We took turns. When it was my turn, I found out that White people's bathrooms were no different than colored people's. Just like Mama, Miz Ruth had one of those fancy towels hanging on the towel bar, the kind of towel that was only for decoration, the kind of towel that nobody was supposed to use. In our house, there was a lacy part on the bottom of the towel. Mama only put that towel out when she was expecting company. Otherwise, it got folded up and put in some secret spot, I guessed, because I never saw it.

The rice got browned, maybe the chicken too, maybe some onions. Whatever they cooked put off such delicious-smelling steam, and my stomach grumbled, like it was ready to be filled again. Mama, Mrs. Jefferson, and Miz Ruth danced around the kitchen like they were old quilting circle friends. Mama and Mrs. Jefferson had different-colored skin than Miz Ruth, but they were the same when it came to the kitchen. All three of those ladies knew how to cook.

I couldn't help but stare, fascinated and amazed.

K-duh. K-duh. K-duh. K-duh. I heard the sound of someone walking onto the porch, and I froze. So did Mr. Jefferson and Deborah. Livvie got still just because the rest of us at the table had turned into statues.

Thursday, June 2, 1921, 5:00 p.m.

The ladies cooking probably didn't even hear, what with the sizzling chicken and the clanging of pots and the chopping of vegetables.

Screeeek! The screen door opened. My head swiveled part-way to see a man who filled the doorway. Right after I got that quick look, I looked away. This house was strange enough. We'd eaten a late lunch at the same table as a White lady. We'd used her bathroom. Now, her husband was coming home to a room full of Black folks? Me staring at him while he walked through his own door seemed too fresh a thing for me to do.

He looked big, from the quick look I got. Not big like he was fat, but tall. I thought I saw brown eyes, and wispy, brown hair that was the color of milk chocolate, but I wasn't sure.

"Somethin' sure smells good," his voice boomed towards us. Hanging his straw hat on a hook by the door, he sent a smile towards Miz Ruth, even though she didn't stop cooking. "It looks like we got some company."

Company? Us? Not an inconvenience? Not people he couldn't wait to get rid of? I couldn't wrap my head around that possibility.

Miz Ruth wiped her hands on her apron and stepped away from the pan she was greasing. "Merrill!" She walked over, and they hugged each other. Pulling away, she nodded to the Jeffersons. "This is Mr. Jefferson and his daughter Deborah. His wife is the one making rolls. That's Henry and Olivia Simmons, and their mom is there browning the celery."

"Well, Mrs. Jefferson and Mrs. Simmons, you two are making the kitchen smell like heaven. I'll be curious to see whether supper tastes as good as it smells."

I snuck glances at Mr. Merrill while he talked. Something bubbled under the surface of his voice, something funny, like he was always on the brink of chuckling when he talked.

Also, I noticed he had lots of lines at the corners of his eyes, like he did lots of smiling and laughing. Maybe he was a kind White man. If he and Miz Ruth both cared about other human beings, no matter what color of skin the human beings had, then it was definitely another first. A White husband and wife who were true Christians? A couple who believed in brotherly love for all brothers and sisters? If this was what Miz Ruth and Mr. Merrill were, they were the first ones I'd ever met.

That evening, we all crowded around the same table, everybody's elbows and hips mixing in with the hips and elbows next to them. A couple of folding chairs were brought up from the basement, and Mr. Merrill, along with the rest of us, discovered the food tasted just like it smelled: delicious.

There was something weird about the meal despite its tastiness. Nobody did too much talking. First, the

Jeffersons and us were trying to catch up, eating-wise, so we were too busy chewing and swallowing to chat. Secondly, just about the minute we sat down, Miz Ruth said something strange that made us all kind of take in a sharp breath, then Mr. Merrill said something strange too, and then we all got silent.

"You know, it was the weirdest thing. In the middle of the night I woke up, and I could see these people moving across our yard. I couldn't see who they were. I just saw their outlines." She put down her fork and shook her head, like she couldn't even believe it.

"Then I heard these words, as clear as a church bell ringing on Sunday. I heard the words, 'Help them.' Isn't that something?"

The rest of us murmured "Yes, ma'am" and "uh huh" and tried not to look too startled.

"I think it was destiny. I think you folks coming down the road past our house—I think it was meant to be."

Mr. Merrill then chimed in with his odd talk and the story of the cots Miz Ruth had mentioned earlier. "Yeah, and a while back I got the idea to make some cots. No reason I could think of. It's not like we were planning on having a bunch of relatives over, but I couldn't shake the idea. It was like a mosquito buzzing. It just wouldn't quit until I up and made them cots."

After supper and after everyone took turns using the toilet, Miz Ruth had Mr. Merrill put our wagon in their garage, and she took us down into the basement and got us set up for sleep. We each got a pillow or something to use for a pillow (I used a folded-up towel), a sheet, and a blanket or quilt. "Sometimes the basement gets mighty cool, even when summer's right around the corner," she said.

The cot wasn't wide enough for me to roll over, but all in all, it wasn't too uncomfortable. After everything that had happened to us, I certainly wasn't gonna complain about a thin blanket or a pillow that wasn't plump. Sure, it wasn't as nice as sleeping on a real mattress, and it certainly wasn't as comfortable as my old bed would have been, but I didn't sag down like I thought I would. Apparently when Mr. Merrill made them, he stretched the canvas til it was extremely taut. In fact it was stretched so tightly, it was like laying on a soft shelf if shelves were ever soft.

After I'd been lying there for a while, not able to drift off to sleep, I said, "Mama, are you awake?"

"Mmm hmm."

"All that's happened to us, Mama, who's going to tell about it?" I whispered it. No way did I want Livvie to wake up, and I also didn't want to disturb the Jeffersons. A small part of me didn't want the Jeffersons to hear what Mama and I said to each other. For almost two days, we'd not even a moment where it was just the two of us. Right then, I wanted to say something just between us.

The rustling of her sheet and the creaking of the cot told me Mama had perhaps shifted, so she could face me. "What do you mean?"

"Well, somebody wrote down everything that happened to Jesus and made a book out of it. The Bible. Who's going to put what happened in Greenwood into a book?"

"Henry, I don't know who's gonna write that story. Who do you think should write it?"

I thought about the time a couple of years ago when I spoke in front of the whole congregation at church. At school, we all had to write a report on a historical hero, and some of the kids chose biblical characters. I wrote about David and his fight against Goliath.

Pastor Jenkins asked me to read my report one Sunday. When I sidestepped past Livvie, Mama, and Daddy and out of our pew, butterflies flapped around in my stomach. Not a sound filled the sanctuary except for the sound of my shoes, stepping down the long, wooden aisle toward the pulpit.

My shoes sunk into the thick carpeting, as I walked up the three stairs to the altar. It was just three steps, but when I got to the pulpit, I felt like I was towering above everyone else; when I looked at the sea of faces in the congregation, I felt like any minute I would topple over.

I stared at my report, then the crowd. Opening my mouth to speak didn't do any good. No sound came out because my mouth was as dry as a desert during a drought.

The crowd must have figured out I was scared because after standing there like a statue for almost a minute, I heard a couple of "Preach it, Henry," and "Speak the truth, son."

What if I couldn't get out a single word? What if my nerves were going to be victorious over my writing?

Then I remembered David. He was smaller than his opponent. He was weaker than Goliath, and yet, he still was the victor. David's story made me realize I might be weakened by my fear, but I could still emerge the winner.

And win I did. I overcame my anxiety about speaking in front of a crowd; I read my report; and when church was over, a bunch of church members found me outside on the parking lot and told me how much they liked what I had written.

Black people were the Davids in this battle. The people of Greenwood were fighting Goliath. Would David get back up and win, despite getting knocked down?

Maybe for our strength to grow, all we needed was our story to spread. I was only twelve, too young to write a book, so perhaps somebody else would write a book about the horrible things that had happened to Greenwood.

"Mama, I don't know who should write the book. Maybe me. Someday, maybe I will tell our story." I stared at the ceiling, as dark as the walls and the corners of the basement. The inky surroundings gave me no clues about the future.

More rustling.

"I think that will happen someday, Henry. That is, if it's what you want. Dreaming and hoping are powerful things." Mama sighed. "But Henry, no matter how much we hope for some things, we have to understand they might not happen."

More creaking. I couldn't see her, but I felt her, as she leaned over towards my cot and circled one arm around my shoulder and her other arm under my head. I could smell her. Mama always smelled like a spice. Nutmeg? Cinnamon? Even if she hadn't baked anything in days, that fragrance still followed her.

"Son, I'm worried about your daddy. I know we've both prayed, and we're not going to quit hoping, but we have to be prepared. Your daddy might be real hurt.

There's no telling what he got himself in the middle of." She got off her cot, kneeled down, leaned over, and gave me a kiss on the side of my head. Her lips lingered for a moment.

"I know Daddy is such a strong man, and you think nothin' could harm him. But honey, he's a man. He's just flesh and bone. He might come back to us with a broken leg or some sore we need to tend to. He might have seen things that are so horrible, he won't want to talk about them." She ruffled my hair. "I just want you to be prepared, Henry, for whatever shape he's in." Mama gave me another kiss and then padded back over to her cot and lay back down.

"Try to get some sleep, Henry. It's been a rough couple of days for us." It wasn't too long after that I heard Mama softly snoring.

Daddy with a broken arm or leg? Daddy with a wound that needed cleaning and bandaging a bunch of times a day? It was still Daddy...

Friday, June 3, 1921, 6:15 a.m. and through the rest of the summer of 1921

The next day Mama called her sister in Kansas City. Miz Ruth and Mr. Merrill let her use their phone and even left the room while Mama made the call. It was a small island of private time surrounded by a sea of very un-private time.

I wasn't sure what my aunt said, but I could imagine what she was saying on her end. Her sister was just as strong and kind-hearted as Mama was. When family was in trouble, everybody on the Simmons side and the Robinson side stepped up without hesitating one bit.

I watched Mama grip the phone, as her knuckles lost a bit of their color, and I thought about how difficult this was for her. She had to say aloud to someone else that she needed help. Mama was fierce in her independence. Relying on other people besides Daddy wasn't in her nature. Saying that she couldn't do it on her own, that we couldn't do it on our own? Those were hard words for Mama's mouth to form.

"Camille. It's me." To anybody else, she probably sounded fine, sounded normal. Only Daddy or me or my auntie could have heard the ragged edges to her voice.

Margaret! I have been so worried about you. How are you? How are the kids? Is everybody okay? That's what Aunt Camille probably said. It was certain that Greenwood had made the papers, and most likely, there were people all over the United States worried about loved ones who had lived in Greenwood.

"Henry, Olivia and I—we're fine."

Perhaps Aunt Camille said, "I am so happy to hear that. Wait. What about James? Is James hurt?" She was sharp enough to catch onto what Mama did not say. However, maybe my auntie said more than that because Mama was quiet for a long time. I watched. Her face changed from having no real expression to a crumpled mess. The corners of her eyes turned down. The corners of her mouth dragged down. And then tears flowed down her cheeks.

"What's wrong, Mama?" Livvie said.

Mama rubbed my sister's shoulder and gave her a halfway hug with her free hand.

"Let Mama talk, Liv," I said, as I put my arm around my sister and pulled her away a little to give Mama some space.

"James?" Finally, she said something in response to whatever her sister had said. "Camille, I don't know. James left to see if he could help with the trouble at the courthouse. He never came back." She rubbed her eyes, drying and smearing the tears at the same time.

"I don't think he ever will come back to us, Camille. I think he's gone."

I imagined Aunt Camille responded, "Oh Margaret. I am so sorry. I can't imagine. How awful." My aunt knew what Mama meant by "gone" because she knew my daddy. Daddy wouldn't have taken off and left for another woman or another life. He wasn't the kind of man who would have left us alone simply because he was looking for a way to get out of his responsibilities.

Gone? Gone meant dead.

Aunt Camille and Uncle Wright drove out to pick us up. They must have dropped whatever they had been doing, and my uncle must not have gone into work because they came later in the day.

When we stood on the front porch and said goodbye to Miz Ruth and Mr. Merrill, Miz Ruth actually took Mama's hand in hers when she wished us well. "I'll be praying for you and your family, Miz Simmons." She then hugged Mama.

Mr. Merrill nodded at Mama and Livvie, and then he shook my hand. I made sure and gave him the same strong grip he gave me. Daddy had taught me well—a man held onto another man's hands with a firm confidence during a handshake. It's a simple gesture, but meant so much. "Take care of these two gals of yours, Henry." As our fingers lingered together, our arms pumped our hands up and down; I felt a current running down from Mr. Merrill's arm and up into mine, then it coursed through my body and warmed my soul.

Mr. Merrill had done what my daddy had for as long as I could remember. He'd made sure we were safe and fed. At that moment, Daddy was with me in the body of Mr. Merrill.

Aunt Camille and Uncle Wright got out of the car. The doors creaked open and thudded shut after they had unfolded themselves out of their seats. My aunt smoothed out the wrinkles in her dress and patted her hair back in place with a few fingers. I figured Mama wanted to run out into her arms as soon as she saw her sister, but that would have been disrespectful to the two people who were standing on the porch with us. Proper goodbyes needed to finish up before we left.

We all nodded at each other; Mama, Livvie and I thanked Miz Ruth and Mr. Merrill and then we just stood there. What should we have said to a couple of people who saved our lives, who gave us shelter in a raging storm of hatred?

I had no idea, and I guessed Mama didn't either.

As we walked across the yard to the car, Miz Ruth cried out, "Oh! Your wagon!"

I twisted my mouth into a half smile and half frown and raised my eyebrows at Mama. I supposed the wagon had been my responsibility to remember. We didn't have any suitcases or satchels to hoist into the trunk. Mama had her bag, and Uncle Wright offered to put it in the trunk. But Mama politely refused, making sure it was securely looped over her shoulder.

"Thanks anyway, Wright, but I think I'll just keep it safe with me."

What was in that bag? Why couldn't Mama let loose of it while we were on the road? What was in there that needed to be kept safe? I was on fire with curiosity, but I figured that at some point soon, when it was the right time, Mama would tell me.

I looked down, making an inventory, and saw I had the extra sweaters and jackets draped over my arm. The only thing missing: Livvie's chariot.

I started to walk back, but Mr. Merrill insisted he would get it, and he headed to the garage. He met us on the driveway, and when Uncle Wright opened the trunk, Mr. Merrill lifted the wagon and carefully set it into the trunk. He closed it himself, then patted the trunk.

As we backed out, the three of us waved. Even though Miz Ruth had asked us to keep in touch, to let them know how we were once we got to Kansas City, I figured it would never happen, but I hoped it would. I hoped we'd send at least a couple letters back and forth. I know folks have great intentions to stay close after they move away, but it hardly ever happens. Miz Ruth and Mr. Merrill had helped us in an incredible way. We might not even be alive if it hadn't been for them. If Miz Ruth hadn't called out to us, one of those trucks full of troublemakers might have found us... and then who knows?

All I knew was even though our time together was brief and even though we'd never see those two people again, we'd never ever forget them.

There wasn't much talk on the ride except from my sister. Livvie and I rode in front with my uncle. The holidays and reunions when I'd seen him, he wasn't much when it came to conversation. That late afternoon, he was even more quiet. Or at least he would have been if given a choice.

Of course, Livvie didn't give him that option. She made up for everyone else's silence. She chattered the whole time. Since she was so short and since she was sandwiched in the middle between me and our uncle, she missed some of the sights. However, the billboards were high enough for her to see and she commented on or asked questions about most of them as we flew by.

"What's that one for, Henry? There's a camel. I know what camels are."

"Liv, that's a cigarette company."

"Oooh, look at that one, Henry. That one has a little girl on it."

"Yeah, that one's for a brand of stove."

"Look at that big bottle of ketchup. Are there really bottles of ketchup that big?"

I leaned against the car's door window frame and let the wind rush across the side of my face. "I don't think so, Livvie."

Sometimes she took a break from pestering me and then she'd bother Uncle Wright instead. "Uncle Wright, do you have any toys at your house?"

In my head, I rolled my eyes. My aunt and uncle didn't have any children. Why in the world would they have toys?

"Olivia, I don't think we have anything you'd call toys. But we do have playing cards, and I know how to play all kinds of card games."

That intrigued her. She wiggled around in the space we were crammed into. Her rear end bumped into mine, as she tried to twist around to face him. "I don't know how to play cards. What games do you know how to play?"

I felt sorry for him. My uncle might have thought my sister would forget this conversation, but he would have been wrong. She wouldn't. Livvie was like a dog with a bone fresh from the butcher. When we finally would get to their house, the minute we walked through the door, Liv would probably be turning her head completely around looking for the deck of cards, so that she and our uncle could play.

Mama and Auntie sat huddled in the back. The way Mama was curled into her sister and the way my auntie was holding onto Mama, it was hard to tell where one of them ended and the other one began. Every time I twisted around to sneak a glance, it just looked like one mound of hair and wrinkled-up fabric. The two of them had their faces nestled into each other's necks so I didn't get a chance to try and guess how Mama was doing.

Sisters. They seemed to be able to talk to each other without words, like they had an unspoken language that only involved their eyes and their thoughts, like their heartache arced back and forth between them like an electric current. I could feel the sparks even though they weren't making a sound.

Was that only something that happened between sisters? When we got grown up, would Livvie and I be that close? If something awful happened to my baby sister, would I hold her in my arms, and would she melt into me like Mama melted into her sister?

I hoped so. After what the three of us had seen, after what we'd lived through, I felt closer to Livvie. It was like we had been forged together by a blacksmith. Our fear and our close calls had heated us up until we were red hot, and the death we'd witnessed had hammered us together. The three of us were now one.

It was too long of a trip for Livvie to stay up the whole way. At some point, the rhythm of the bumps in the road, and it getting dark lulled her to sleep. I tried to keep her slumping towards me, so Uncle Wright could drive without Livvie asleep on top of him. With the black sky surrounding us, everybody in the car got quiet. I looked out the window at the stars and wondered how hard it was going to be for Daddy to find us. Like Harriet Tubman, would he use the stars to guide him on his journey back to the three of us?

When we got to my aunt and uncle's home deep into the night, we settled in as best we could. Mama slept in their extra bedroom. Livvie and I camped out in the family room. Aunt Camille piled up quilts and afghans to make us comfortable.

As the days wore on, my sister and I played together a lot more than we'd done in a long time. It was summer, and we didn't know any other kids. I supposed we could have wandered around outside until we happened upon some neighborhood kids and probably that would have led to a ball game or a game of tag, but it just didn't feel right. Livvie and I hung around in the house, or sometimes we went into the backyard and wandered around, kicking the dust up in the bare spots and walking in big circles that never met up, or played with Buster, their dog. We ate meals with my aunt and uncle, but it didn't feel right. It didn't feel like we were truly living.

One of my friends had told me about purgatory— the place between Heaven and hell—and that's where I felt like we were. We weren't in our old home. That was probably gone forever. But we weren't in our new home either. In fact, it didn't feel like it was our home at all. It was like we were stuck in an in-between place, and we were walking around on our tiptoes, trying to be as quiet as we could be. Oh, don't think my aunt and uncle squashed us down and made us feel like we were a bother, that we were unwelcome. They didn't. They did the best job they could to make us feel like their home was our home—for as long as we wanted.

For a while, we stayed. But it was like the old expression about waiting until the other shoe drops. Mama, Livvie, and I were waiting for the other shoe to drop onto the floor. One shoe had already thumped to the floor. Daddy was gone. We were anxious about what would happen when the other shoe hit the floor. What would life be like without Daddy? I wondered.

Mama hadn't given up hope entirely. I knew she was keeping a tiny ember burning because whenever the phone rang, Mama jumped a little. Maybe in her heart she was thinking that it was Daddy calling, that he'd been hurt, but he'd finally gotten to a phone, and now he was eager to get our family reunited.

Also, when Aunt Camille went out to the mailbox and got the mail, Mama's eyes darted to whatever handful of envelopes my auntie brought into the house. Was there a letter in that bundle from Daddy?

Livvie would ask, "When's Daddy coming to get us?"

"Why is it taking Daddy so long to get to Uncle Wright's?"

"How long before Daddy gets here?"

I guessed Mama figured it was finally time. One night as Livvie and I settled on top of our cloud of covers, Mama came in and told my sister to come sleep with her that night. Then, I didn't know what the two of them said to each other, but the next day, Livvie's bottom lip was quivering, and tears were spilling out of her eyes. I found out what they'd talked about.

"Henry, Mama said that Daddy might be in Heaven right now." She stared at me. Was she hoping I'd tell her that Mama was wrong?

Of course I couldn't do that. "I think Mama's right, Livvie, and you know, Heaven is a wonderful place. God is taking good care of Daddy."

She bit her lower lip. "Mama said that Daddy's watching over us right now. She said he can see what we're doing, and if I want to, I can talk to him when I say my bedtime prayers." Her face tilted up towards mine, unmoving.

Leaning down, I kissed the top of her head. Finally, all the times Mama had promised that Daddy was going to find us soon, that we were going to see him any day crumpled into a pile of burning-hot sorrow. Most of me had known for a while that Daddy was dead. Him being gone while we'd made our way through Greenwood didn't make me lose all hope. I figured he was caught up in the mess at the courthouse. Him still being gone when we left Greenwood and stayed with the Phelps still left me hopeful, too, because he had no idea where we'd be if we weren't at home.

But now? Now we'd been at Uncle Wright and Aunt Camille's for a couple of months. By now, if Daddy was still alive, he would have called the other family members, one by one, until he'd found us.

In my head, I'd known for a long time. For a long time, I'd known he was dead. But in a small corner of my heart, I'd kept a chunk of hope alive. Now, all hope was gone.

At night, when Livvie and I huddled around with Uncle Wright and listened to radio shows, Mama and Aunt Camille would sit at the kitchen table and talk. Snatches and snippets would reach my ears, so I knew they were talking about all sorts of things but mostly, they were figuring out what Mama could do. Mama had never worked before. She'd taken care of me and

Daddy, and then Livvie and me and Daddy. She was determined to take care of Livvie and me again. In her own place. In our own place.

After staying there for most of the summer, the three of us moved into an apartment close to my aunt and uncle. Aunt Camille had her own seamstress business. One night at dinner, Aunt Camille talked about Mama working for her.

"I always got too much work and not enough time in the week to do it, Margaret. You'd be helping me out." So it was decided. Uncle Wright paid for our first couple of month's rent, and he also bought a sewing machine for Mama.

The apartment? It sure wasn't as homey as our house, but given time, I knew Mama would put her own touches on the walls and with the furniture to make it look like the Simmons lived there. She looked and looked until she found a nice place that came furnished since we had nothing but some clothes.

Mama slept on the pull-out sofa. Livvie and I each had a tiny bedroom, and the sewing machine, with its lid closed, was a side table in the evening. During the day, the lid was lifted up, Mama's foot pedaled and pedaled, and the machine whirred and whirred. She liked her job for two reasons. One, she got to stay home so in case I got sick or Livvie got sick, Mama could tend to us. Two, she liked being able to support us on her own. Even though Uncle Wright tried to argue with her, he was no match for my mother. She insisted on paying them back a little something every month and even kept a notebook to make sure she paid the debt in full. Mama was the heavyweight champion of determination and independence. Always was and always would be.

And that bag that Mama had carried from Greenwood to Miz Ruth's house and then to Kansas City? The mystery bag, full of pointy things that made me curious about the contents but also made me patient about finding out what was inside it? Mama had kept the bag in her room while we'd been at Aunt Camille and Uncle Wright's, and then when we moved into our own place, it sat in the corner by Mama's sewing machine for a few weeks. One night I got up to get a glass of water before going to sleep, and I found Mama at the kitchen table, the bag on its side in the middle of the table.

My glance that darted immediately to the bag and my raised-up eyebrows must have told Mama I was busting at the seams to see inside that bag.

"Henry, did I ever tell you what I'd packed in this bag before we left?"

I shook my head. "No, ma'am."

Mama patted the seat closest to her and said, "Have a seat. I'll show you."

Finally.

She reached in and carefully pulled out a framed photo and held it against her. The image faced me. I'd never seen the picture before.

I leaned closer. "Is that—"

"Yes, it's your daddy and me when we were just dating. We went to a photography studio in Greenwood on a lark—it was only in business for a year or two—and sat waiting while another couple picked up their pictures. Your daddy and I almost couldn't hold in our laughter at their fussing. The man had yawned, and the woman's eyes were closed. Those two were not happy about it. But they refused to pay to get another photo made, so they were stuck with it."

Mama turned the picture around, so she could look at it. "When it was our turn, we wanted to make sure our eyes were open when our image was captured. Daddy told me, 'Let's open our eyes wide, like we're lookin' at a ghost, and let's smile real big with our teeth clamped together like we're one of those ventriloquist's dummies,' which of course made me laugh." She set the photo down on the table. "I kept it in my sweater drawer. When I felt like an old and tired mama, I'd take it out and remember how young I used to be."

Mama pulled out a small metal box. The outside was decorated with yellow and red flowers, but the paint was chipped in places. Mama lifted the lid and rifled through the white cards that were crammed in there.

"This is my mama and my grandmother's legacy— the family recipes I grew up with. Bread pudding. Peach cobbler. Pot liquor soup. Hush puppies. Of course, after I'd cooked and baked these dishes many times, side by side with my mama or my grandmother, I didn't need the written-down directions anymore. But I keep 'em because just looking at the recipes, in their handwriting, reminds me of wonderful times."

The recipe box was set down, right next to the framed picture. Mama then rooted around, feeling for something small, it seemed like.

"Ah, here it is." In her hand was a bracelet. It had gray things dangling from the gray chain.

"This was the first sweet gift your daddy got me. He said he picked this one out because it had a spool of thread on it. Little did he know that once you kids came along, most of the sewing I did was mending and darning." She slipped it part way onto her hand and made it jangle. "It has a cat on it. I never did have a cat. It has a fake diamond ring. I never was interested in a flashy ring. But it caught your father's eye, and he loved me enough to buy it."

Mama then turned the bag upside down and at the same time, she reached into the bag. A book slid out into her hand.

"Henry, the other things—the charm bracelet, the picture, the recipe box? Those are from my past. But this—" and Mama held the book up against her chest. "This is from the present and the future."

She opened up the book as I scooted my chair right next to hers. It was a homemade scrapbook. Mama had taken a drawing book and taped something on each page.

On the first page was a story I'd written in first grade. After I'd showed it to Mama and Daddy, I never saw it again. I figured they had thrown it away. Apparently not.

As Mama slowly went through the book, page by page, I saw how I'd grown as a writer. There were silly, childish poems that used rhyming words in an awful way. There was a copy of my report on David fighting Goliath, along with a program from church that day. There was my name, printed in bold, black ink.

In that book was everything I'd written so far in school. The earlier stories included drawings, and I had to chuckle over some of them, as Mama and I took turns pointing out funny things. The people's hands were as big as their heads. I colored the sky white and the clouds blue. The dogs looked like sausages with long legs like a horse.

We looked at the last report that was taped in the book and then she closed it. I noticed there were many blank pages following my poems and stories. Would Mama keep filling it up?

I shook my head. Why had she taken the time to save them like this? I had to ask.

"Mama, these were just things I wrote in school. What made you keep them in a scrapbook?"

She ran her hands along the top of the book. "It wasn't my idea. It was your daddy's."

I leaned back in my chair and my head went way back. Daddy? Daddy being impressed by my little-kid poems and reports? "Daddy? Really?"

"When you were still in diapers, your daddy dreamed about you as a grown man. He didn't know what you'd do with your life, but he did know one thing. He knew he wanted you to be more than a mechanic."

Mama cupped my chin in her hand. "Don't get me wrong, baby. Your father was never ashamed of the work he did. Not one moment. He repaired cars to the best of his ability, and he always did it honestly. But for you and for Olivia, he had bigger dreams. He wanted each of you to make a difference in the world."

Tears trickled down my cheeks.

"Maybe you'll be a doctor or a lawyer. Perhaps you'll be a teacher or a writer. Maybe you'll decide to be a musician or a ball player. Whatever it will be, your daddy wanted to keep track of the path you took. He wanted to celebrate your accomplishments all along the way."

Looking at the collection spread across the table, I realized that even though he was gone, Daddy would always be keeping an eye on my journey. The things in the front of the scrapbook weren't anything to be proud of. However, I looked forward to filling up the rest of it with writing that would make even Daddy puff up with pride.

October 1921

It didn't take too long for me to make new friends. My school was alright, I guessed. My algebra teacher didn't explain things enough, but I found some math-smart kids who helped me. The gym wasn't as nice as the one in my old Greenwood school, but I was more into baseball than basketball, so the small court didn't bother me too much. One teacher, however, made me want to go to school every day—Mrs. Murray, my English teacher. That first year we lived in Kansas City, I wrote more than I'd ever written before. It was like my pencil had been dammed up, and finally, out onto the paper flooded pages and pages of words. Mrs. Murray was built like a fire hydrant, but even though she was shorter than me, she was tough. That year, I learned I was a writer, and I realized I had stories to tell.

Back when summer was still hanging on, Uncle Wright and Aunt Camille had driven us back to Greenwood. We spent the night in a colored motel that was not quite in the colored part of town but sure wasn't in White Tulsa either. We wanted to see what had happened once we left town. We wanted to see if anything was left of our old neighborhood.

We shouldn't have bothered.

Uncle Wright took his time driving. When we pointed and cried out things like, "Look. That's where the Dreamland Theatre was!" he'd slow down or stop. There wasn't anything to see, however. The big pieces of burned-up buildings had been hauled away, somewhere. All that was left of the businesses were black rectangles of space and smaller pieces of charcoal. Charcoal that used to be wood frames and doors and ceiling tiles. Chunks of junk that used to be restaurants and grocery stores and barber shops.

We drove down street after street, block after block until we got to our house, or where our house used to be. Like everything else—like Daddy—our home was gone. Mama stared for a moment and then turned her head away and refused to look. Probably she was just like me, hoping that our home had somehow managed to survive. To see the truth was too much to take.

Rolling past all the open spaces where houses used to be brought back memories. Just a few months ago, I batted some balls with Daddy. He tried to pitch some fastballs and curveballs, trying to get me to swing and miss, but when his fast balls came in slower than molasses, he laughed at himself, and I laughed right along with him.

Just a few months ago, I hung our wash out on the clothesline, the bleachy clouds rippling through the air, as the sheets danced in the breeze.

Just a few months ago, I played Red Rover with a bunch of friends in our backyard. Two lines of kids, their hands locked together, as one by one we tried to barrel through with enough force to break the chain.

Now it was nothing but memories.

70 years later
Spring 1991

When I got to be eighty-something, I went back to Greenwood, and this time I brought along my book and my granddaughter.

My book really began when I was still a kid. Back then, we sent a few letters to Miz Ruth and Mr. Merrill, and exchanged letters with the Jeffersons. Deborah and her parents had written to the Phelps, asking for our address. They'd moved a little farther east than us and had settled in St. Louis. Deborah felt about St. Louis like I felt about Kansas City. It was okay, but it would never be as good as Greenwood.

Our letters trickled to nothing within the first year, and then the Phelps and the Jeffersons disappeared from our thoughts, in spite of how important they had been to us. Miz Ruth and Mr. Merrill had shared their home with us after we'd lost ours. After seeing so many White people do such horrible things to Black people, the Phelps had been kind.

And there was no way for Miz Ruth and Mr. Merrill to know what we'd endured, but the Jeffersons knew. They had cried tears over the same things we did. They had the same hole in their hearts that we did. Just sharing the basement and sitting at the kitchen table with them, and being able to look into their eyes, knowing we'd survived the same horror—well, it gave us hope. Both our families survived the massacre. Both our families had a future.

When they vanished from our lives, I wondered about all the other folks who had disappeared because of the massacre. Some had been killed. Some ran out of town like we had. Some were forced to live in tents in Greenwood parks until they could rebuild their homes. Who was going to tell their story?

For about ten years, I pecked away, telling the story as best I could. History books didn't even mention the Tulsa Race Riot. Just the term alone made me laugh. It wasn't a riot. Black folks didn't go crazy and start tearing things up, all out of control.

No sir, it was a massacre.

Mama, Livvie, and I only knew what we knew. We'd only seen what we had seen, so for the last ten years, I'd had to hunt down the people who'd seen it all. Person by person, witness by witness, I pieced together what had happened during those awful two days.

Like those airplanes I'd heard as I hunkered down in my bedroom. I had no idea what they'd been up to, but lots of other Greenwood folks knew.

Louella Montgomery said the planes looked like "maniacs grinning, as they dropped kerosene bombs on us." We talked on the phone, complete strangers when the conversation began. By the time we hung up, we were acquaintances, connected by something so horrible, it was almost beyond belief.

She said the high-pitched whine, so close to the ground "was a warning scream. As they crisscrossed our neighborhood, it was as if the pilots wanted to kill every Black person they saw. So many bombs dropped from the skies, the sidewalks were covered with the burning balls."

Toward the end of our talk, I apologized for making her dredge up those terrible memories. When I'd read the quote somewhere that "writers live life twice," I knew that meant the painful parts as well as the pleasant parts. Mrs. Montgomery had witnessed awful things back in 1921. As I asked her questions, as we talked seventy years later, she was reliving those horrendous moments.

"Oh, it's alright. The nightmare of the massacre is never buried too deep. And the worst thing, for me, wasn't the destruction and the death that the planes brought about." Even over the phone, I could hear the trembling in Louella's voice as she finished. "What makes my heart ache the most is for the first time in the history of the United States, Americans—on American soil—were being bombed by airplanes. And it was being done by other Americans."

As I was doing research, I dug up an article that included what Homer Ragsdale saw as he hid under a bridge. Homer was just a teenager in 1921—not much older than I was back then. From what he said, a truck puttered up the curving road. Black bodies were stacked up like cordwood in the truck bed. As the truck headed across the bridge, Homer stepped out from under the shadow of the trestle to get a last look before the truck crossed the bridge and disappeared around the next turn in the road.

But it didn't cross right away. The driver stopped halfway across. He and another White man got out and started dumping the bodies off the bridge.

The article included a quote by Homer. "Those men didn't say a word. It was like they were doing some chore, like dumping the trash, and just wanted to get it done, so they could go home and have dinner.

"One after another, I saw them drop from the bridge. Some landed flat, smacking the water with a splash before tipping down and then disappearing. Others pierced the surface of the river like knives. The Arkansas River immediately swallowed those bodies. Right away, they vanished in the brown current."

What Mama and Livvie and I had lived through had been swept under the rug for decades. What Louella Montgomery and Homer Ragsdale saw and heard, that all got hidden and then forgotten. That bothered me. Part of the word history is story. When people forget the stories or they never get the chance to hear the stories, they don't get the whole picture. Maybe they only get the White people's version. Maybe they only get the racists' version. If that's so, I wanted to add my voice, so that my story blended in with everybody else's.

It's a terrible thing to be someone that other people wanted to destroy—all because of the color of my skin.

I wrote down what I remembered and got it published myself. I knew that's not what most folks did. Most folks wrote something and sent it off, and they tried to get an editor curious.

I have limited time. I'm old. My primary goal was to get the story told. I didn't care if anyone else was interested in my story. I was interested. Still interested. Whenever I was able to sit and rest myself, I'd travel back in time to Greenwood. Why had the White folks dropped kerosene bombs on us? Did they regret burning down a whole city? Just knowing that Tulsa's skeletons were being dragged out of the closet was enough for me.

I went to libraries and schools peddling my book, which I ended up calling *Greenwood Gone: Henry's Story*. Everywhere I traveled, I had a box full of those books in my car trunk. After all, you never knew when you might encounter someone who wanted to buy your book.

Viola, my granddaughter, wanted to see my childhood home through my eyes, so she was my chauffeur when we went to Tulsa. We did lots of walking. I pointed out things that were no longer there. Vi took pictures and asked questions. Some houses had been rebuilt in the old style from my childhood. A couple of churches had risen up, triumphant, from their former ruins.

We spent one of our days in the Greenwood Cultural Center. Viola, a couple of times, had to call me back to the present. "Grandpa. Are you okay?" she'd ask when she found me transfixed in front of one of the huge photos on display. It was like I was in a fog. It felt like my blood slowed down and settled sluggishly in my legs and feet, rooting me to the spot. Being able to go back to 1921 made all the joyous as well as the sad moments come rushing back.

So much loss. The new shops and restaurants now along Greenwood Avenue were nice little places and all, but they didn't have the character of the old shops. The new places were glass and metal, but I didn't see much heart. At least not the heart I remembered from when I was a boy.

The Greenwood of my childhood, up until the massacre, was an idyllic place. I traveled the town from corner to corner and back again and again and always,

I felt safe and loved. The business owners. Our neighbors. Daddy and Mama.

Daddy with his huge hands—hands that could fix anything with wheels and hands that could soothe any ache we had. He did his best to protect us until the night he left us and never came back.

There were times those first few years in Kansas City when I got mad at Daddy. If only he'd stayed home with us, we wouldn't have lost him. We wouldn't have had years of not knowing.

For me, that's what haunted me the most—the not knowing. Livvie and I didn't talk much about it, but there were occasions where we'd speculate.

"Maybe he got shot trying to keep the mob from getting Dick Rowland."

"Maybe he was killed by one of those kerosene bombs they dropped from airplanes."

Whatever happened, I hope it was quick. Losing Daddy was bad enough, but the thought of him suffering? That was almost too much to bear.

Eventually, pride blanketed over my teen-aged anger. Instead of being enraged that he'd left us for good to help someone else, I saw the bigger picture. Daddy was trying to make the world a better place for Livvie and me. He worked at the garage so that our home was a place of peace and protection, and when he left that night to help stop a lynching? Well, that was him again trying to keep the love and safety in Greenwood and keep Tulsa's hatred and racism out.

Over the years, I'd learned it took courage to stand up when a flood of hate was coming right at you. Daddy loved us with a fierceness that's still with me, but even though he didn't fight back when he was called a boy and he didn't lash out when White people spat on him, as they passed him on the sidewalk, he couldn't stand by when an innocent boy was about to be lynched.

Maybe he saw my face when he thought of Dick Rowland? Maybe he wondered who would stand up and try to save me if I was ever in danger like that?

And Mama? Mama was just as fierce as Daddy. She refused to let us lapse into lazy, slang-filled talk. She didn't let up when it came to my sister and me doing chores to help keep our home running smoothly. Mama protected us from danger, no matter how overboard she went. She'd light into me about my grades and refuse to accept anything but my best. When my friends would come over, they'd always jump back when Mama got on my case. They were afraid she'd go after them, but I'd say, "Don't worry. Mama's bark is worse than her bite."

Maybe our bite should have been fierce and maybe our bark should have been so loud, people all over the country could have heard us. Maybe if we had been ferocious and bitten back when the little transgressions came about, maybe Greenwood would still be the safe, friendly place I was lucky enough to grow up in—at least for part of my childhood. I do think about that a lot. Was there anything that could have changed the course of history back in 1921? Could anything have warmed the cold hearts of the White people who killed our neighbors and burned our houses down?

I wonder...

The end

Dear Reader,

I'm a teacher. I've spent years writing alongside students like you while teaching them how to share their stories. Together, we've drafted and revised memoirs—stories that are based on the memories of our lives. I believe with all my heart that sharing our experiences empowers us. Our feelings—our very existence—are validated by speaking the truth of who we are.

What happens when that truth is not told? What happens when memories never have the chance to surface? What happens when voices are silenced?

When I was writing the first draft of this book, it was merely a piece of fiction. I did research. I created a plot. I made up the Simmons family. When the story came to the final line on the last page, I felt satisfied. Sort of. I didn't know that I wasn't invested yet. I did know, deep down, that *something* was missing.

Getting feedback from someone is priceless. I was lucky enough to find a talented editor and after my editor (she's also now my publisher) gave me specific advice, I scrapped my first draft and began again. Almost immediately, it wasn't me telling the story. It was Henry. Sounds weird, right? But it's true. It was if I was just a scribe, typing away on my keyboard while Henry told his story. This has never happened to me before.

Henry and I come from very different backgrounds. But having a character speak to me and having that character steer the story—taking it out of my control—is something that's never happened to me. In my opinion, it happened either because all the voices from 1921 that have been silenced all this time are finally speaking up—or there really was a Henry Simmons, and he's finally being heard.

Sincerely,
Sioux Roslawski

Selected Bibliography

I f you are interested in reading more about the Tulsa Race Massacre, here are some resources that the author used during her research:

Carlson, I. Marc. "Timeline of the Tulsa Race Riot." personal.tulsa.edu. http://www.personal.utulsa.edu/~marc-carlson/riot/tulsatime.html

Christensen, Linda. "Burned Out Homes and History: Uncovering the Silenced Voices of the Tulsa Race Massacre." zinnedproject.org. https://www.zinnedproject.org/materials/burned-out-of-homes-and-history-the-tulsa-massacre

Ellsworth, Scott. *Death in a Promised Land: The Tulsa Race Riot of 1921*. LSU Press, 1992.

Ellsworth, Scott. "Tulsa Race Massacre." okhistory.org. https://www.okhistory.org/publications/enc/entry.php?entry=TU013

Johnson, Hannibal B. *Black Wall Street: From Riot to Renaissance in Tulsa's Historic Greenwood District*. Eakin Press, 2007.

Johnson, Hannibal B. *Tulsa's Historic Greenwood District*. Arcadia Publishing, 2014.

Keyes, Allison. "A Long-Lost Manuscript Contains a Searing Account of the Tulsa Race Massacre of 1921." smithsonianmag.com. May 27, 2016. https://www.smithsonianmag.com/smithsonian-institution/long-lost-manuscript-contains-searing-eyewitness-account-tulsa-race-massacre-1921-180959251/

Krehbiel, Randy. "The Questions That Remain." tulsaworld.com. https://www.tulsaworld.com/app/race-riot/timeline.html

Mullins, Dexter. "Survivors of Infamous 1921 Tulsa Race Riot Still Hope for Justice." america.aljazeera.com. http://america.aljazeera.com/articles/2014/7/19/survivors-of-infamous1921tulsaraceriotstillhopeforjustice.html

"Tulsa Race Riot Timeline." tulsaworld.com. May 31, 2016. https://tulsaworld.com/news/local/tulsa-race-riot-timeline/article_a69f47d8-febb-51bf-b800-950bce097c42.html

ACKNOWLEDGMENTS

I read a novel recently, and the author (Celeste Ng) said a reader asked her why she had thanked so many individual people (sixty-five) in her acknowledgments. I thought I had her beat, and I was right. Hopefully, I did not leave anybody out. If I did, I apologize.

This book would not have been born if not for the following seventy people (I think I counted correctly):

Thanks to Caiti Quatmann, Elizabeth Yee, Nellie Quinn, and Caroline Hackmeyer. You ladies helped keep me true to the character Henry from the very start, you encouraged me when I was just beginning this project, you gave me constructive criticism when the much-necessary transitions were nonexistent, and you made me wonder: What *was* going to happen to the Simmons family? Would they all survive? Honestly, it was something I hadn't considered—until our retreat at Toddhall.

And speaking of Toddhall? You folks fed us and gave us a lovely place to write. All we had to worry about was getting words down on paper. I always looked forward to our retreats at your center. Thanks for giving me a seat I could sit in and write for hours and hours on several weekends.

The National Writing Project—and more specifically the Gateway Writing Project: You helped nurture me as a teacher of writing, which of course led me to becoming a better writer. Diane Scollay, Myrtho Prophete, and Michael Lowenstein—you made me take part in the SI, and you made me love it. Nancy Singer and Katie O'Daniels—you made sure I had more opportunities along the way, and for that, I'm grateful.

Darice Murray—Thanks for letting me know I *can* tell this story, that this white-as-notebook-paper writer has permission to tell this story because, after all, it's my story, too. It's not my story of rage and sorrow and loss, but it *is* my story of regret and embarrassment. And hopefully, with this story being told more frequently, the storytelling will eventually lead to further healing.

Thanks to all my 2016-2017 students at St. James the Greater in St. Louis—Ryan Mataya, Cameron Cohen, Mikayla Murphey, Emily Durgin, Clarady Brooks, Danny Hochstatter, Madison Pitts, Elizabeth Keeley, Dierdre Bolan, Brandon Pitts, Anthony Ryan, Nathan Swederska, Phillip Keeley, Cameron Lanemann, Aidan Lanemann, Calder Bailey, Kayla Cummins, Caitlyn Cordia, Amaya Marion, Joseph Lang, Joe Morgan, and Nolan Worley. You, ladies and gentlemen, pushed me forward and prodded me to write every day during NaNoWriMo of 2016. Without your nudging and your daily presence next to me, I probably would *not* have taken on this project, or I for sure wouldn't have felt the need to finish it. For you young people, I am eternally grateful.

Danny Hochstatter—Out of all the students, I'm indebted to you the most. Even though you hated to read and you avoided writing whenever possible (don't even try to tell me it's not true), you encouraged me. Every month or so you'd ask, "How's that story of yours coming along, Mrs. R?" or "Have you finished it?" When I'd admit I was stuck, that I was still writing it, that I still wasn't done with it, you'd shake your head ever so slightly, smile, and let me off the hook... until the next time you inquired. That gentle prodding made me determined to see this story through til I ran out of road. Thanks, Danny.

Thanks in advance to my writing peeps—Linda O'Connell, Tracy Brosch, Lynn Obermoeller, Kim Lehnoff, Katie Krushaar, Tim Woodcock, Stephanie Gavin, Rebecca Carron, Terry Baker, and Jen Ferguson. You writers pored over my writing— sometimes shorter pieces that served as digression— and kept me writing on a regular basis.

Thank you, Amanda Bramley, for offering to be a beta reader. The knowledge that you were waiting for this manuscript to be finished nudged me along and kept me from procrastinating (sometimes). Sometimes the procrastination won. And Linda O'Connell—you also generously offered to be a beta reader, and you read my manuscript over the course of one night and gave me confidence that it had some merit. Thank you.

Bob Miya, Anne Wright, and Greg Gates—back in the 1970s, you put up with me as an overalls-wearing, angst-filled, rebellious student. The three of you taught me the power of words along with the importance of doing the hard work when it comes to writing. You were bright stars (along with Dian Simons) at Hazelwood West. Thank you for becoming teachers.

Thanks to two gentlemen, one at the Tulsa Historical Society and Museum and the other at the Greenwood Cultural Center. Ian Swart, you gave me access to a 1921 Red Cross report that helped me piece together some of the specifics that happened in the aftermath of the massacre. Also, thanks to Bill White, at the Greenwood Cultural Center, for sending me some links, along with being so kind when I visited Tulsa. You invited me into your office and were so friendly and informative, and all the while your dinner (sitting on your desk) was getting cold. Thank you for being so hospitable and so generous with your time.

Joanne Lozar Glenn. If you had not suggested starting a writing accountability group, I am close to positive this book would not be here. Because of your nudge, I got nudged and prodded and had my butt royally kicked for two years by the Butt-Kickers. Thank you for your wonderful advice. And to the Butt-Kickers: Nicole Pyles, Sue Bradford Edwards, Renee Roberson, Angela Mackintosh, Ann Kathryn Kelly, and Kelly Sgroi. You rough and tough ladies didn't give up on me even when I worked at a slower-than-a-snail's pace. Thank you, thank you, thank you.

To my French sister Virginie Desplain: You published a book first, which spurred me along. Thanks for being such a wonderful and talented sister. To my half-sister Nancy Bennett: I know it's not our birth mother's story, but Henry's story was clamoring to be told. Thanks for encouraging me along the way.

To my two friends who I've loved since middle school, Tricia Speier and Richard Kennison. You were and are my oldest and dearest friends. Because of you two, I'm certain that West *was* best, and you two are the best.

Thank you to my maternal grandfather, Cecil Spurgeon. Grandpa, you were born in 1904, and it was your sayings and slang that I sometimes heard as I wrote this. I hope I got the era close to right.

Riley, DaShawn, and Pete: You make me want to be the best person I can be. Riley—I hope you enjoy this book (a little). DaShawn and Pete: One day, I hope you find this book on your bookshelf, and I hope you have enough curiosity to crack it open and start reading. (I also hope you read it, Virginia, and that you're proud of my effort. Ian, I know there's not enough car chases and shooting for it to appeal to you. Just know your mother had enough determination to follow it through to the end.)

Margo Dill, because of you, this story is (hopefully) not a meandering and lackluster story. Because of your spot-on editing skills, this tale blossomed. You are a gem among editors. If this book shines at all, it's because of you. And then, unbelievably, you said, "I'd love to publish your book," after you started your own

233

press. Without you, this manuscript would be still gathering dust...

Thanks to Linda Christensen. You inspired this book. Until I took a workshop of yours, I had no idea this piece of history was woven into our country's fabric, only to later be shoved under our nation's couch. I imagine I would still be ignorant of it, if not for you. I hope I did a halfway decent job of carrying the torch for a short way.

Michael—Finally. I did it. Thanks for your encouragement even though you yourself have only read six books so far. (I'm okay with that because one of them was George R. R. Martin's *Fevre Dream*.)

And finally, the biggest thanks. Imogene Gann, you gave birth to me...and then you surrendered me because you knew you weren't fit to be a parent. Carol and Ollie Kortjohn, you were the best parents a kid could ever ask for. Thank you for putting up with all my teenage angst and my rebellious ways. I grew up okay—because of you. I'm just sorry the three of you aren't still alive to celebrate with me.

ABOUT THE AUTHOR

Sioux Roslawski is a St. Louis middle school teacher, a freelance writer, and a teacher consultant for the Gateway Writing Project, a part of the National Writing Project. Contact her via her website: siouxroslawski.com.

Please note: All of the author's proceeds from **Greenwood Gone: Henry's Story** *will be donated to benefit the residents of Greenwood. The publisher will also be making regular donations from the proceeds of the book.*

If you liked Henry's story, and you would kindly write a review on the site where you purchased this book, we would really appreciate it. Reviews help readers find books they will enjoy and learn from. Thank you for considering!

ABOUT THE PUBLISHER

Editor-911 Books publishes entertaining and informative books for children of all ages and adults, specifically writers and parents. Owned by Margo L. Dill, we are located in St. Louis, MO, and on the web at Editor-911.com. The three imprints under Editor-911 Books are Editor-911 Kids, Editor-911 Fiction, and Editor-911 Knowledge.

To find out more about Editor-911 titles, you can sign up for our newsletter at Editor-911.com on the Editor-911 Books' page to get updates and a free picture ebook, *Maggie Mae, Detective Extraordinaire: The Case of the Missing Cookies*, delivered right to your inbox!

Check out other middle-grade titles from Editor-911 Kids:

- <u>Only My Horses Know</u> by Cinda Jo Bauman
- <u>Anna and the Baking Championship</u> by Margo L. Dill
- <u>Finding My Place: One Girl's Strength at Vicksburg</u> by Margo L. Dill
- <u>Read-Aloud Stories with Fred Vols. 1 and 2 Collection </u>by Fred Olds (These stories are middle-grade reading level.)

Made in the USA
Monee, IL
29 December 2021